GEORGE REYNOLDS, O.P.

THE
COBBLER AND THE
CRICKET

AND OTHER TALES OF
FAITH

NEW PRIORY PRESS
EXPLORING THE DOMINICAN VISION

Chicago

Editor: Paul Byrd, O.P.
Copyeditor and Designer: Marie Pabelonio
Illustrator: Robert Reynolds

ISBN 978-1-62311-003-1

For my sisters Marty and Sandy,
And my whole Dominican family.

Contents

The Cobbler and the Cricket

In a far away country, in a far away time, there once lived a poor cobbler. And he was very poor indeed. He lived in a very poor house, no more than a hovel. He had his work space with his leather cutting tools and his needle; he had a cot with one very thin blanket against the winter winds; he had an ancient table upon which he cut his bread when he could buy any; he had one chair with only three legs because he had to burn one leg in the hearth last winter. Now the cobbler was so poor that if he did not get paid for his labors when the work was delivered, he would have no money to buy thread for the next pair of shoes he must repair.

But what could he do? He could not take the villagers to court because he could not afford a rich man's justice. When the lawyer brought shoes to be repaired, he told the cobbler the rich people could not be taken to court because the rich people were his friends. And when the parson brought his shoes in to be repaired, he told the cobbler that he could not mention anything about poverty in the church because the rich people would be offended and surely, the cobbler would not wish to offend the rich people. When the mayor brought his shoes in to the cobbler, he said that the cobbler should be proud to know that his mended shoes would be on the mayor's feet on the high occasion of the parade, which celebrated the liberation of the town from its oppressors.

So if we tell the truth, we must say that the townspeople considered the cobbler not only poor but also something of a fool. They did not pay him for his work until they chose to and they did not bring him their shoes until the shoes were almost nothing more than mere shreds of leather that held the tops to the soles. Then it was almost impossible to fix the shoes and the rich townspeople would scoff at the cobbler's work and tell him he was not a good cobbler, but a loafer and they would not pay him for his labors. And so, one by one, the townspeople remembered less and less how much they owed the cobbler for his work, and they remembered more and more how the cobbler should delight in their business because they were rich and important people.

But the cobbler did not consider himself poor. In fact, he felt very rich. For besides the table and the chair with three legs, besides his cot with the one thin blanket, and besides the work space with his cutting tools, he had a cricket. And the cricket was a fine cricket indeed. He sang his simple song to the cobbler to wake him in the morning. He sang his simple song in the afternoon to keep him working at the shredded shoes. And he sang his simple song in the evening to keep the cobbler company as the light drifted towards the West. When the last light had faded, he sang his simple song so that the cobbler could fall asleep upon his cot with the one very thin blanket.

The cobbler talked to the cricket and told him everything that he was thinking. "I do not think we will have customers today, Little Cricket," he would say. Or, "Perhaps today, Little Cricket, since the day is so fine, someone will come and ask for shoes to be mended." Or, "I think the rain will keep people away from our door and then we will have nothing to eat tonight. I hope, Little Cricket," he would add, "you are not too hungry today." And each time the cobbler spoke to the cricket, the cricket answered with its simple song and the cobbler, even when he was hungry, would smile and feel very rich and happy.

The cobbler never complained. After all, he had a roof over his head although the roof leaked, and he had a bed to sleep in although it was only a cot with one thin blanket. And he had his cricket that listened to him hum as he worked, and heard him whistle when he finished a pair of shoes, and heard him snore when he went quietly to bed.

"How rich I am," thought the cobbler. "I do not need a large bin for my wheat nor a large pot in which to store my milk. I do not need a big table on which to mend the shoes because the shoes are always small. I do not need a large closet to keep my one blanket and I do not have many clothes so I do not need a dresser to hold what I do not have. I am indeed," he said to the cricket, "a very rich man." And the cricket answered with his simple song.

Now it happened that one night the cobbler did not sleep well. Instead of the comforting dreams he usually had, he dreamed of strange lands and strange people; he

3

dreamed of dark pits and falling trees; he dreamed of erupting earth and dangerous horses. When he awoke, he knew that something was wrong, but he could not point to the wrongness. He looked at his table and saw all of his tools where he left them; he looked at the chair and saw it was just as he had last used it; he looked back at his cot and saw that it was exactly where it had always been. But still he knew something was missing. But who could steal from such a poor man? Suddenly it came to him: what he was missing was the sound of his cricket! The silence in the room hurt his ears and confused him. Where was the simple song of the cricket? Why did he not answer when the cobbler called?

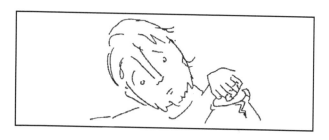

Then he looked by the hearth, and there was no cricket. He looked under his work bench, and there was no cricket. He looked at his cot and shook the one thin blanket, and there was no cricket. He looked into his broken milk jar and in his small wheat bin, and there was no cricket. "Where have you gone to, Little Cricket?" The cobbler called. And there was silence in the room. The only sound the cobbler could hear was the beat of horse hooves on the street and the shout from the children that the mayor, a very important person, was riding by.

"Are you still asleep, Little Cricket?" The cobbler asked in the empty air. But he could never remember a time when the cricket slept longer than he did. "Have you hurt yourself, Little Cricket?" The cobbler asked. But still there was no answer. And then he thought aloud, "Little,

4

Cricket, have you gone for a walk? Yes, that must be it. You have gone for a walk and I must wait for you. Hurry back, Little Cricket, and I will be very quiet as I listen for your song."

The cobbler sat on his one chair with the three legs and waited. He listened for the first hint of his cricket's voice. He dared not mend shoes because he did not want the noise of the hammer nor the noise of the needle pulled through leather to distract him from the sound of his cricket. He waited as the day grew brighter and the sun grew stronger. He waited as the shadows became darker and the road grew dustier. But still there was no sound of the cricket. The cobbler waited without moving lest the rustle of his clothes hide the sound of the cricket's greeting.

But he could wait no longer. "Perhaps, Little Cricket, you have gotten lost and cannot find your way home. Yes, that is it: you have gotten lost. You went for a little walk and got lost. I must go out and find you."

And so the cobbler looked around his home, saw that everything was where it should be, the tools and bits of leather were on the work bench, the chair with three legs leaned against the table, the cot had the one thin blanket carefully folded resting upon it. Everything was just as it should be. The cobbler took one last look and walked out the door.

As soon as he stepped out through his door, he called to his cricket, "Little Cricket, where are you?" He stopped and listened but he heard only the noise of the busy people passing. The horses rushed past, full of power and haste. The merchants shouted out their wares and called to those passing by to come and buy their bread or their corn or their pottery. Little children laughed and ran noisily in their games of hide and go seek. The cobbler for the first time became fearful. Would his cricket be able to hear him call with all that noise? And would he be able to hear his cricket calling to him? He was afraid not to move on so he sat down and leaned against a wall. "Little Cricket, oh, Little Cricket. How will I find you?"

The cobbler sat against the wall for the rest of that day. When it was too dark for the busy people to be on the street and for the children to play their games, he again called to his cricket and listened. There was no sound. He waited for a few moments and then called again. But again there was only silence. "I must remain calm," he told himself. "I must remain calm and notice everything. I must notice all the places that are like the places my cricket liked in our house. I must have the sight of many eyes to see under leaves and behind stones. I must have the hearing of many ears to catch the least bit of sound my cricket made when he spoke to me. I must—," and he stopped himself. "I must move on and look for my cricket."

Fear and the tension exhausted the cobbler. He was

afraid to go to sleep in case his cricket called him in the night, but he was also afraid not to rest because he knew he might have a long journey ahead of him in the morning. Finally sleep won out and the cobbler closed his eyes and fell immediately into a deep slumber. During the night he had another dream. He saw a large hall with many people in it. There were more people in that hall than were in his whole village and they were walking around the hall but they did not seem to be taking steps. It was more like birds going from place to place but without flapping their wings. It was beautiful and bright and warm. And in the middle of all those gliding people the cobbler saw his cricket, sitting all alone on a very high throne as though he were directing the people. As soon as the cobbler saw his cricket, he woke up with a start. "My cricket is calling me," he said. "I do not know where you are but I know now that I will find you."

Light had just begun to fill the deep blue morning as the cobbler rose from the wall he had leaned against for the night. He called once, then twice, then a third time. But the cricket did not answer and so the cobbler began his journey into the dawn. The first person he saw on the road was the mayor.

"Mister Mayor," the cobbler said as he approached this important man. "Mister Mayor, have you seen my little cricket or have you heard him in the night?"

"What? What? Who are you and what are jabbering about?" The mayor responded.

"I am the cobbler who has fixed and sewn your shoes so many times so that you could look elegant and important when you had parades to go to and speeches to give. Don't you remember me? And don't you remember my little cricket? He would say hello to you when you came to my shop and he would greet you as the important person you are and talk to you most sweetly and happily?"

"Ah, now I recognize you and I have some more shoes

7

for you to fix, but I need them right away so get back to your shop. I want my shoes by tonight."

"Mister Mayor, I cannot get back to my shop until I have found my cricket. If you see him, please tell him that I am looking for him. I'm sorry that I will not be able to fix your shoes right now but I will hurry back as soon as I can."

"Such nonsense," the mayor said more to himself and to the air than to the cobbler. "Looking for a cricket! And to think I trusted my shoes to such a crazy man. Bah!" And the mayor walked importantly on.

The next person the cobbler met was the parson as he hurried on the road. "Oh, this is fine," said the cobbler to himself. "He knows everyone around here and he will surely have seen or heard of my cricket. Please stop for a moment," the cobbler said to the parson. "I wonder if you have seen my cricket?"

The parson glowered at the cobbler. "Your cricket? You stop me to ask if I have seen a cricket?" The parson sounded very angry and he frightened the cobbler with his question. "I don't know anything about your cricket, or your wasp, or your gnat, or your bumble bee, or your whatever. If he had gone to church regularly maybe I would know him but I never saw him there so I know nothing about him or if he even exists."

"But my cricket talked to you when you came into my shop to have your shoes mended. He would greet you most reverently and speak most gently when he saw you. Please. Are you sure you have not seen my cricket?"

"You are questioning my word? You miserable man! You should know better than to doubt the word of one as holy as I. Now get back to your shop for I have shoes for you to mend before tomorrow when the bishop comes and I must look my best."

The cobbler said nothing, but he did not return to his shop either. He looked at the parson very sadly and resumed his search. After taking a few steps, he would stop and listen. And then he would call to his cricket. But always there was silence. An occasional bird would call the cobbler to encourage him to continue, and once a fox barked to him to give him hope. But of the cricket, there was only silence.

The cobbler walked until the morning was almost gone. He came to a very poor farmhouse and as he passed by, he heard the sound that seemed to be a little girl crying. At first he wanted to travel on, but the sound of a child crying was more than the cobbler could ignore. He looked in the doorway of the poor farmhouse and indeed there was a little girl crying. She held in her hands a doll that was in many pieces. And the way she was sobbing, the cobbler knew that this was a very precious doll to her. The head was separated from the body, an arm was separated from the shoulder, and a foot hung loose from one of its legs.

"Little girl," the cobbler said. "Do not cry. Perhaps we can fix your doll. Let us see." He took the doll into his

9

hands and turned it all around. The doll was old and had been much loved and mended many times and the cloth could barely hold together the dress or the other arm or leg. The cobbler put his hands into his pockets to find a piece of thread, for that was all the doll really needed was some thread— not much, but just enough to fix the doll so the little girl could stop crying. The cobbler always kept his needle stuck into the collar of his shirt so that it was easy to find it when he needed it. He held the needle in his hand but he could find no thread. He looked even harder and felt deeply into his pockets, but still he could find no thread. Then he too became very sad because he knew that he could easily sew the doll together if only he had a piece—,not a big piece, not a long piece, not a colorful piece—, but just a piece of thread.

"I am so sorry, little girl. I could easily mend your lovely doll, but I have no thread." And then a thought came to him. "My shirt! My shirt has thread. It is old thread but it just might fix the doll and, after all, it is an old doll." So the cobbler began to pick at the sleeve of his shirt until a little bit of thread was loose from the cloth. He picked a bit more and there was more thread. Just before the sleeve would fall from his shirt, he knew that he had enough to sew the head and one arm back on the doll. The doll would not be completely mended, but at least she would be more whole than she was now.

As the cobbler sewed, the little girl stopped her crying. As she saw the head take its place on the body, she began to smile; and as the arm grew back onto the shoulder, she giggled at first and then the giggle grew into a huge laugh. "But I cannot fix the foot, little girl. I am very sorry."

"Oh, that will be fine, Mister Cobbler. I shall always be able to carry my doll wherever she needs to go, but now she can see and she can put her arms around me. You are such a good man and I thank you. Thank you. Thank you." And then she ran, almost danced, out the door with

10

the doll held tightly in her arms.

"Now I must hurry and look even harder for my cricket," the cobbler said to himself. He watched the little girl for another moment and then returned to the dusty road. Soon he was out of sight of the poor farmhouse and his eyes were growing weary from looking at the road and at the stones and at the leaves that covered it. Occasionally, he stopped and called and waited. When he heard no reply, he would continue his journey.

Now it happened that as he was looking for the cricket, he saw a little boy sitting very quietly by the side of the road. He made no sound, but just sat there. In his hands he held a small leather ball, but all of the stuffing inside (or what should have been inside) was also outside in the boy's hands. As he sat there quietly, his face was very sad and looked as if he would at any moment burst into tears. The cobbler stopped and said to the little boy. "Why are you so sad, little boy?" The boy looked from the stuffing and the ball in his lap to the cobbler and said, "My ball is falling apart and I do not know how to fix it."

"Well, let's just see what we can do about that," said the cobbler. He searched through his pockets once more, just in case he missed the bit of thread he would need. But once again he found nothing. So with a sigh, he began to pick at his other sleeve, for by now he knew where he could get at least something to sew the ball together. He picked first at a little bit, then a little bit more, and then just a bit more so that his sleeve did not completely come off of his shirt. He took the ball in hands and the needle from his collar and very carefully sewed the ball together. But he did not have quite enough thread and some of the stuffing would not go back into the ball. "I am sorry, little boy, but that is all I can do."

The sadness had left the boy's face as the cobbler had worked and now it was replaced by a big grin that was so wide even the boy's ears wiggled. "Oh, that is fine, Mister

Cobbler. I can take special care of my ball and make sure
that no more stuffing come out and I can still toss and play
with it. You are wonderful," said the little boy as he ran
into the field, tossing and gently catching the ball with both
hands.

The cobbler smiled to himself and almost laughed out
loud at the antics and happiness of the little boy as he ran
into the distance. He watched and had almost—but not
quite—forgotten about his own loss of the cricket. "I must
search even harder and longer now for my cricket," he said
to himself. "I must listen very, very carefully, for perhaps
my little cricket too is weak and cannot sing very loudly."
So intent was the cobbler in listening for the thin sound of
the cricket, he did not hear the pounding of horse hooves in
the distance. So intent was he in looking at the stones and
the leaves by the road, he did not see the dust the horses
were sending into the dusk. The cobbler looked up just in
time to see the front of a stocky warhorse that threw him to

the ground and then trampled on him. The last thought the cobbler had was, "Now I will never find my cricket and I am more sure than ever that he needs me."

As the darkness deepened, the memory of the cricket grew dimmer and dimmer and the desire to see and hear Little Cricket grew stronger and stronger. The image of the cricket then grew larger and larger. No longer was he simply a little friend who could be held in the palm of the cobbler's hand. He grew so large that he filled the cobbler's eyesight as he had filled the cobbler's hopes. He grew until he filled the cobbler's mind and eventually he filled the cobbler's entire dream.

The cobbler then entered into his dream and he found himself in a huge bright hall with many people drifting around, more people than were in his entire village, and they were all singing. The sound was like nothing the cobbler had ever heard before. It was strong and gentle at the same time; it was soothing and exciting; it was loud and yet did not hurt the ear; it was a warm sound and so sweet the cobbler's eyes began to get teary and his sight was almost blurred. It was just like his dream, only better. It was bright like his dream, but the brightness did not hurt his eyes. It was a more peaceful feeling that came over the cobbler, more peaceful than he had ever known before.

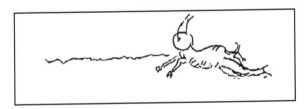

However there was one difference from his dream. In the middle of the large hall, sitting on a high throne was not his cricket but a very beautiful lady, more beautiful than any lady the cobbler had ever seen. All the cobbler could do was to stare at this dazzling person; he could not move

13

and he could not speak. But the beautiful lady could speak and she said, "Cobbler, you have done well all your life and you must be rewarded properly." When the lady began to speak, all of the other creatures ceased their dancing and gathered around her seat in the middle of the great hall and they bent toward her, awaiting her next words. "You may have anything you wish, for you deserve it."

The cobbler, still struck dumb with all of the beauty and splendor around him, could think of nothing to say. And he could not remember a time when he wanted anything and so he could not now ask for whatever he wished. Perhaps he had even lost the ability to wish. But then, as he looked around at all the friendly faces, he did remember something. He remembered that the little girl's doll was not completely mended and that the foot was still missing. He remembered that the little boy's ball was not completely sewn together so that the stuffing might tumble out again. So the cobbler raised his eyes and said, "Perhaps..." All of the creatures around the beautiful lady stopped their singing and leaned forward, not wanting to miss a single syllable of what the cobbler would ask for. "Perhaps I could have...but no, that is too much to ask."

"Please continue," the beautiful lady said gently. "Perhaps you could have...?"

"Perhaps I could have..." He stopped again, thinking his wish would be too great even for the beautiful lady in this grand place.

The silence in the hall became intense, so intense that even the brightness seemed to impel a hushed reverence. The cobbler took a big breath into himself, and fortified with that gift finally said, "Perhaps... perhaps I could have some thread." Then remembering that he could have anything he wished, anything as large as the sea and as precious as gold, he also thought that there might be other little girls and boys there who had broken dolls and toys which he could mend. And so he added timidly, fearful that he might be asking too much. "And maybe it could be a whole spool?"

Then into that vast expectant silence, into that great bright hall, as all the creatures leaned forward and as the beautiful lady looked at the cobbler, came the unmistakable gentle sound of the song of a little cricket.

Romance

This then, will be the tale I promised you. But I should tell you right away that this will be more in the way of a romance than a story with a tidy beginning, middle, and end. We will have neither talking hares nor wounded stags, although there is a dancing bear— and that only briefly and with no advancement of the action. The medieval troubadours would have given up interest before half of this romance was over and those eager for a moral to their stories would have been disappointed to find that the moral is outside the tale and not inside. And I would not want those who are expecting a romance to confuse the tale with the romantic. There is a young cavalier, a beautiful lady, and a comely child. So there is that romance, to be sure… but that is not the romance.

No, this romance is for those who do not confuse the substance of their dreams with the dreams themselves. They do not ask the sunset why it is not a mountain, nor a hind why it is not a lion. Those romantics will learn nothing new, but will recognize what they have known all their lives. And those are the truest romantics of all.

So much for the introduction. Now then, to part one of the tale: it takes place in the remote mountains of a kingdom that no longer exists. And the immediate scene is the abbey which dominates the valley. The valley itself was somewhere between two kingdoms. The border was always a matter of dispute and changed with a war, a marriage, or a treaty in some third kingdom, but it never disturbed the abbey. Only great affairs were recognized within the walls and border disputes were not considered material for great affairs. There were occasions when wounded soldiers appeared at the gates of the abbey, having left a battlefield. And other occasions, a whole army would march past, smart and trim on their first appearance, torn and ragged on their return. But little changed within the abbey walls except that the prayers for the dying and the dead became longer and the chests of the apothecary became more or less depleted.

The abbey itself was dedicated to St. Genesius, the patron saint of actors. There was a legend that after his death, St. Genesius had traveled through this valley with a troupe of actors. Our Lady had granted them their one request that they be allowed to perform together in a final

17

show with all the best actors and actresses then assembled in the anteroom of heaven. It was to be a performance that would entertain her Son as He waited quietly for the time He could return to earth. They performed for Him. The birds and the rabbits gave their finest performance too. And, in gratitude, Our Lady welcomed them into heaven. And as a memorial, the animals and birds provided a perpetual supply of food for those who lived in the valley. When the small band of brothers came looking for a place to found their abbey, they were granted a vision of St. Genesius and his troupe on that spot and had stayed in peace and quiet for their entire history.

And always there were monks to tend to the business of being monks. No matter what happened outside the abbey walls and the valley, the lilt of Gregorian chant mixed with the golden peal of the abbey bell in the cutting air of winters and the crystal air of summers. No one came there to find Paradise, and no one stayed because he had found it. The Psalms of early morning and the songs of birds answered each other antiphonally that the whole world might know that human plots and plans are always tentative and subject to a more compelling wisdom.

The century of our romance is far less important than the day, for it is on the first day of the village fair that events began. The abbey opened its gates each year to all those who wished to sell what their labors had produced over the long winter months. The mountain passes were barely cleared of snow and the crocuses were just beginning to bloom on the eastern side of the hills. Lent was yet one full week away. One began to feel the fair in the bones before it was felt in the air. The children sensed the preparation before they saw the packing and they immediately renewed their Christmas resolves of goodness and obedience. Even the threat of missing the fair was enough to bring the most recalcitrant to heel and virtue.

The erection of the booths was as carefully planned as

any battle by any general in any history of conquest. Bits of ribbon and cloth were hoarded lovingly against the moment when they would dance in the breeze of the abbey courtyard. There were tightly woven shawls stacked in neat piles beside tightly woven baskets of various sizes and colors. Painted dishes, fired while bread was baking in the same oven, were arranged like a millipede with wheels. Dried and decorated gourds were carefully carved and hung from string that hung from carts which showed their age and the station of their carvers. Little and large figurines, delicate and gross, whittled from pine or oak or elm, were lined neatly on shelves, a litany in wood. Brightly colored booths lined the entrance of the abbey and it was though the whole of the year-long monastic silence had erupted into one gigantic burst of color and energy.

And the people! Everywhere, there were people. One knew there were merchants who lived in the town, farmers out in their pastures, and shepherds in their meadows. One also knew that families grew below the thin trace of smoke that rose on a windless morning. But to know they were

19

there to see them was all the difference between a thought and its consummation. Some looked like the retired military men they were, standing aloof but completely engrossed in what their wives and children were doing. Others were the taciturn shepherds who carried the meadows in their hands and the long nights of watching sheep in their eyes. Still others, the farmers, stood stolidly like the trees they uprooted, arms crossed like entwined branches, and weighed to a nicety the value of their cheeses and beef.

The only strangers allowed were the traveling circus performers from the south. In honor of St. Genesius, the people dared not deny a place for those who threw heavy sticks and kept five of them magically in the air at once, or those who dressed in exotic costumes and recited the lines from strange plays which no one there understood, or those who — and now we come to the dancing bear — used a small switch and forced the huge animal to stand on its back legs and keep rhythm to a drum and tambourine.

It was as though the peace and order, enclosed within ritual and discipline, had exploded into a bounteous original chaos.

From his window, high above the courtyard and distant from the involvement of commerce, stood the Abbot. His age was indeterminate. When there was crisis in the abbey or when he was asked to make a difficult decision, he could have been the same age as the saint they venerated. But when he was alone, accompanied only by the angels in his prayer, he could have been the youngest novice seeking entrance to vows. But on this day, the day our story begins, he appeared to be a man straddling the vigor of middle age and the sagacity of the elderly. He had seen the fair many times before and had always thrilled to the vitality below him. It reminded him of nothing but itself, a feast for eye and ear which displayed the infinite variety of the infinite God. He remained immobile, like a wool sponge soaking up the atmosphere, not moving lest he disturb the delicate balance of sensations engulfing him.

He knew that he would be called on shortly to give the blessing which opened the fair. He could not do it too soon, for the people needed time to view the wares and pick out those special objects which they would demean with their lips in the act of bartering for. They would covet these in their hearts with the pent up lust of isolation which could fasten quickly on the one thing their imaginations needed most for them to endure the coming winter. Nor could he wait too long, for the outer limit of patience is the same boundary as the inner limit of violence and more than one

21

skull had needed attention when the bartering had been held at bay. And to begin the exchange without the blessing would have been as unthinkable as missing the fair altogether.

Eventually the inevitable knock came at the Abbot's door. The porter, Brother Guillam, opened the door and stood silently, waiting for the invitation to speak the words they both knew would be spoken. "Yes, Brother?"

"They are ready, Father Abbot."

"Ah, yes. Well, let us go."

And only the two of them knew with the certainty of faith that the curtain was officially being raised on the annual festival of human folly about to be played out before them.

This then, ends the first part of our story as the Abbot leaves his cell and walks down the stone steps to join the commerce of the world of people with the blessings of the world of God.

II.

The stairs which the Abbot and Brother Guillam hurried down were steep and dark, for they were used only infrequently. There were no torches lining the way with sulfurous vapors and the cobwebs did not take kindly to the damp within the enclosed stone passage way. The walls were dank with an ancestral chill which emanated from them, and how could it be otherwise? For this stairway led directly from the Abbot's chambers to a small door in the courtyard and was used only on this annual occasion of the fair.

At the time the abbey was built, there had been rumors of strange tribes with pagan customs who were waiting to slaughter the black robed builders and reduce the abbey to rubble. The architect, a brother whose name is now known to God alone, more fearful of the tribes than his vow of stability and trust in the Lord, had designed a stairway for escape should escape ever be necessary. In the course of time, the tribes and the customs vanished and escape was no longer part of the monastery's thinking.

But still the Abbot and his faithful domo were the only habitual users of the stairs, and they used them only on this one day of the year. For them, it was not that the stairs were sacred, or mysterious, or filled with fear and omens. It is just that the stairs were not needed at other times.

The two monks emerged from the stairway into the light and noise of the fair, and were again momentarily stunned by the freshness of the air and the sounds and the colors. It took them several deep breaths and several blinks of the eyes and several shakings of the heads before they could allow themselves to become part of the panoply which surrounded them. They were recognized immediately and those closest to them began to greet them with loud and exaggerated civility. Those in the nearer distance heard the greetings and they too joined in. And then those in the farther spaces picked up the fever of anticipation that the fair was soon to begin, so they added their shouts to the growing din of merriment and soon the whole world sounded as though the mountain might fall in the blast of welcoming the Abbot to the fair.

With a great dignity that he reserved only for high liturgies and official visitations, the Abbot stepped into the crowd and smiled broadly at all of the merchants gathered around him. He nodded with a solemnity he feigned for their sakes at each one of the townsmen, for inwardly he felt the same excitement and thrill of novelty as did they. He handled their wares, inspected the scarves and the cheeses and the baskets and the reeds and the pots, made suitable comments to each one and then blessed each booth and its occupants with special words of appreciation and invoked the proper saint's protection.

He missed no one and failed to notice nothing. At a glance he could tell whose eyesight was failing, and therefore whose shawls were not quite as good as they were last year. He noticed when an amateur carver had passed into the realms of professionalism and might be asked to work on the choir stalls in the abbey. He felt sadness when he saw that the straw in a basket was not as tight as it was last year and that the hands that wove it were gnarled and stiff. He smelled the cheese which told him that the goats had been well tended and fed with dried clover over the long winter past. He looked at each booth and knew immediately whether the good Lord had lavished blessings on the inhabitants or whether He was preparing them for a higher reward in the next world with increased suffering in this.

The fair was not to begin before the last blessing had been given, but the whisperings behind him told the Abbot that he had better not take too long with the invocations as he neared the end. Since those in that part of the courtyard were the last to enter, they could not expect the same care and attention as the early arrivers. So there was neither jealousy in a shortened formula, or feelings of being shunned as the Abbot got to the last booth. Finally, he spread out his arms and announced to all those at the fair, "My friends, may the Lord bless you all and give peace and prosperity to your labors."

Immediately there was a surge of movement from one place to another and loud shrieks of delight split the air. The ritual of disdain for a treasure had begun and the long and pleasant haggle of price inaugurated. It was confusing, and disturbing, and wonderful. It was the whole world in a moment which would take a whole lifetime to assimilate.

There are always forces, seen and unseen, at work in our universe. There is the force of the sun which soaks fresh life into the grass in the spring, and the force of the mallet which helps the sculptor liberate the face or the hand or the gargoyle from the stone. There is the force of the wind which shapes trees into places of shade and places of security in the storm, and the force of the storm itself which washes and cleanses the air of its summer heat. And there is the force of the dog which holds the wolves at bay, and the force of the moon which causes children to be born. To some, that force is Nature, to others God, to still others Fate. But to all it is a recognition that our arms are not strong enough, nor are our eyes sharp enough, nor are our ideas big enough to encompass all that we touch or see or think.

Since we have seen the Abbot so firmly in charge of the festival, so completely respected and needed by the people, so secure in his power as Abbot that he could set the valley kingdom in motion and ordain its orbit, it is time to introduce our antagonist. And notice please, from the beginning, that he would not have recognized himself as such.

And is that not usually the case? Two desires, both commendable and reasonable, are in conflict and a contest of wills ensues. Or the casual word at a banquet sets two great houses against each other. Or a small piece of grazing land becomes double-claimed through usage by neighboring shepherds. Neither one nor the other knows at the time what powers are lurking, waiting to erupt into hostility. Or conversely, what powers are dormant, waiting to be awakened into the creative force that will weld two families together in a marriage or a pact of peace. Antagonist and protagonist are not always enemies, but may really be the two lingering notes of a reed pipe that spread harmony over a feast like a benison. Or they may be the two sides of an unthinkable desire that, when joined, become the beginning of an unbearably beautiful dream.

We live quite well without our enemies. But we die, bit by bit, without our antagonists. They exert a powerful force over our souls which makes us rise to heights we would not dare, or they elicit our cowardice and make us run from the demons of self-knowledge that have haunted us from birth.

Just such an unnamed force is now at work on our Abbot. As he had walked from stall to stall, he became aware of a strange sensation of being watched. Obviously every one at the fair was looking at him and that is not what I mean. He felt he was being watched. That there was someone behind him or before him who not only heard the blessings and saw the sign of the Savior being made in the air over the wares, but someone who noticed every move and gesture of the ritual, someone who penetrated it and understood the meaning, someone who saw the man behind his office.

The Abbot felt somehow inadequate at the pull of that force. His movements became more deliberate and his words more commanding as he somehow felt a power being drained from him. As he raised his head to see if he could espy the source of his uneasiness, he was greeted with nothing but eager faces or greedy eyes or hands that held special artifacts for his notice. He smiled as he walked through the throng but his heart was missing from his eyes. He could not escape the feeling that he was being judged and for something (a blessing? a crime?) which he could not name.

No, it was not being judged as much as being tested, that was it. He was being tested and his soul was being held in a suspended balance of acceptance or rejection. But by whom and for what he could not imagine. He knew only that his life was being pulled in all directions at once and that his past and his future were mysteriously both present.

Nowhere that he looked could he find the source of his confusion. He glanced over his shoulder, nothing; he looked ahead, nothing; he stood on his toes to see those farthest away in the crowd, nothing. His uneasiness grew as he walked back to the abbey door.

And there it was.

Standing in front of the lintel was a youth, not quite child and not quite man, dressed in shabby clothes and holding a pilgrim's staff. His hat was soft and stained with many days of sweating in the sun and his eyes peered from under the brim with a steadiness and unflinching strength which compelled attention. His jacket was just now becoming too short for his growing body. The look on his face was one of expectancy, as though the rhythm of the fair was merely a prelude to the fugue of his and the Abbot's encounter.

The Abbot halted as though struck deaf and dumb, and indeed for him it was as though the fair had vanished and with it his power of speech. He knew he had never seen the lad before and yet the very presence of the lad had drained him of thinking and feeling. He felt the force and his own inability to withstand it. He felt pulled into a meeting which his whole life had left him unprepared for and yet which his whole life had led him to.

It was the pilgrim who spoke first. He had walked up to the immobile Abbot, his voice gentle and unused to speech, his demeanor respectful and ignorant of arrogance. "Father Abbot, may I speak to you?" The Abbot could say nothing. He heard the words but their meaning did not penetrate. He could only continue to look into the youth's eyes and be held as a butterfly fixed upon a pin for closer examination. "Is something the matter, Father Abbot? May I speak to you?"

With an effort that called forth the same power that led Saint Peter from the dungeon, the Abbot blinked several times, shook his head to clear his mouth for speech and answered, "Yes, of course." But he did not recognize his voice. It was as though the words came from some distant mountain peak but retained their comprehension in the clear mountain air. "Yes, of course," he repeated. "Come with me."

The Abbot led the youth through the abbey gate, through the courtyard, and into the abbey church. It was the hour of Terce and the monks were intoning the opening psalm:

How good God is to the upright;
The Lord, to those who are clean of heart!
But, as for me, I almost lost my balance;
My feet all but slipped.

The words of the chant rose in measured cadences up to the abbey roof, and then through the clouds, past the heavens, and then into the very throne of God Himself where they played before the Divine Majesty and brought back healing peace for those who sang them.

For me, to be near God is my good;
To make the Lord God my refuge.
I shall declare all your works
In the gates of the daughter of Zion.

The Abbot and the youth waited until the monks had finished and the last reverberations of the chant had faded in the distant vaults of the church. They watched the solemn march of the monks and heard the faint whisperings of the robes as the church became empty of all life save the flickering candle hard by the altar. It was the Abbot, now more firmly in charge of himself and more secure after hearing the chant, who spoke first.

"Well, now. What can I do for you?"

"Father Abbot, I want to join your abbey."

The Abbot waited, but there was nothing more than the simple statement. It was as though once the words had been spoken, there was no need for discussion or information or report. The words themselves carried their own execution and fulfillment and anything more would weaken their reality.

The two sat in silence, the Abbot looking at the flickering light of the candle and the young man looking at the Abbot's face. Had the youth the art, he could have read a war raging in the Abbot's mind and soul. But he had not the art, so he waited quietly for the Abbot to speak. At last, the Abbot tore his eyes from the candle, looked directly into the youth's eyes and asked, "Do you know what you are asking?"

The answer came quickly and without hesitation. "Yes, Father Abbot. I want to spend the rest of my life living in the abbey and doing the will of God."

"And do you know enough of the world that you can with such simplicity ask to renounce it?"

"I do not know how much of the world I know, but I know enough to know that I want to spend the rest of my life in the abbey, doing the will of God."

Obviously, thought the Abbot, he has prepared himself for that question, which was to be expected. But there was something in the answer that bespoke an ingenuousness which acted as a protection from attack or trial or even from further questioning.

The Abbot cleared his throat and spoke, more to himself than to the lad. "Many young men come to the abbey to do the will of God and many leave because they find His will is not here for them. Some come seeking God and find they have left Him in the fields. Some come to answer a need they have to know God better and they find that knowledge of God has eluded them. Some come to leave the cares of the world behind and they think they will find a safe shelter from life's storms; instead they find a raging torrent in their cells and so they too leave.

Others come to lose themselves in anonymity because they are too well known in the world for their crimes, or their appetites, or their power. They find that what they

30

have run away from is waiting for them here. And those who do find God learn that He is not what they expected, so much more loving and yet so much more demanding. Sometimes almost cruel. And there are some (here the Abbot's voice grew very faint and was less than a whisper) even who come to escape God."

A long silence followed the Abbot's words. Neither moved. Neither did they almost breathe. Finally the Abbot added, "Here we are not wise, nor clever, nor patient, nor even holy. We know only that the search for God or the escape from God is God Himself."

The Abbot stayed, lost in his thoughts, seeing something beyond the abbey church and even beyond sight. For several long moments he was present only to a distant memory. Then he shook his head, as one who might be emerging from some dangerous land successfully traversed. He asked so quietly that the boy almost did not hear the question, "And does your mother approve of this request?"

"I think she would approve, but I do not know for she is dead."

The Abbot looked at the lad and said the single word, "Come."

The two walked swiftly from the church, confusion on the boy's face, determination on the Abbot's. They came forth from the cool quiet of the church into the noise and color of the fair. It took them a moment to adjust to being again in the world of traffic. But then the Abbot put his hand on the boy's shoulder, pointed him to the middle of the crowd and asked, "What do you see?"

The boy was puzzled as much by the Abbot's words as he was by the sight before him. No, it would be more accurate to say that he was more puzzled by the words than the sight. Although never fully at peace, he had always existed in that world he now viewed and the words were both very familiar yet somehow threatening. He looked at the moiling crowds for a difference, or a strangeness, or an

unfamiliarity which he could detect, but he found nothing.
The Abbot's hand on his shoulder gripped him more firmly
and once again the Abbot asked, "What do you see?"

"I see people and their wares. And I see many colors
and lovely booths. And I see little children running between
their parents' legs. And I see circus performers and
jugglers. But I do not know what you want me to see. Is
there something that I am missing?"

"I do not want you to see anything that is not there."

"Father Abbot," he pleaded, "can I not join your
abbey? This is what I want to leave behind when I do the
will of God. I want to join the other monks at their prayers
and get up early and eat in silence and work in the fields
and listen to the lives of the saints. Can I not," he repeated,
"join your abbey?"

The Abbot did not answer the question. Instead, he looked squarely into the boy's eyes and said, "I want you to join the circus performers for a year and a day. You will do what they tell you, you will eat what they offer you, you will work as they command you. On this day tomorrow, one year hence, if you still wish to join us in the abbey, you may return. For now, go: and go with God."

The young man could not hide the disappointment from his eyes, which became glassy with tears or his voice, which became unsteady and slightly quivered. "Yes, Father Abbot. A year and a day." His shoulders were slumped as he made his way slowly through the crowd. The Abbot watched him as he walked away, tears forming in his own eyes as he felt a mysterious power going out from him at the same time there was a strange strength filling him. He knew he had made the second most important decision in his life and he knew, for the second time, that his life would never be the same.

III.

Now that we have come to the end of our second part, we have to stop a moment and decide what our third part will be, for the chronology of history and the chronology of life are seldom the same. For some, their destiny or the meaning of their lives is found in a providence that impels them forward. Their vision is fixed behind them and they fulfill that destiny, feeding on the source of what they have seen. They are like the pearl diver who has watched a precious gem slip into the sea, and although he cannot recapture it, he knows that it is there and he feels rich in that knowledge.

For others, it is the opposite. A mystical, indefinable intensity lures them forward to a distant point which they can neither discern nor escape. They are like a mountain climber who knows only that he must find the source of the echo which rings in his ears and beats in his heart and will give no respite or surcease. The knowledge which consumes him is the knowledge that no other sound will be as sweet, no other quest as important. It is he who feels the morning star before he sees it and who thrills to the tune before the musician plays it.

So our third part must deal with one vision and our fourth part another. I shall take the mountain climber first, and that as you may have guessed is the boy. His restlessness is more than youthful vigor and desire for adventure. In all things measurable, he is normal and undistinguished from other lads his age. But in the heart where all the important qualities reside, he might well be a changeling, snatched not only from another time but also from another world.

His request for admission into the abbey was as honest as it was ingenuous. He had tried to tend sheep in the hills, for he loved to watch the new born kids playing in the deep grasses and nursing so confidently at their mothers' side. And as he watched them, he knew he was missing something important and could not rest in his contentment. He had tried to work in the fields and he loved to watch the grains he had planted sprout and grow in the springtime rains and mature in the summer sun. But it too was not enough and the harvest left him feeling strangely incomplete and lacking. He had tried making pots for the villagers, and he loved to feel the moist clay in his fingers and he marveled as new shapes emerged from the formless mass into works of beauty and loveliness. But no matter how beautiful the pot or how exquisite its shape, it was not enough.

It was then that he felt if he could but join a monastery, he would find what he had sought in the lambs and in the fields and in the clay. So it was with a mixture of deep disappointment, bordering on despair, that he left the Abbot's side and made his way to the circus performers. He truly did not hear the sounds of laughter around him nor did he notice the little children bumping into him. He was as oblivious to his surroundings as he was to his destiny at this moment. With an effort that cost him dearly, he pulled himself back into the fair and approached the leader of the performers.

"May I join you," he asked, "and help you with your circus? I will work hard; I will be honest and not steal; I will treat your animals kindly and feed your bear daily; I will mend your pots or make you new ones; I will help you tend your children while you are performing and I will ask for no pay other than a place to sleep and food to eat. But I must return to this place in a year and a day without fail or I shall surely die."

The master of the circus stared at the unremarkable-looking boy in front of him and heard his quite remarkable request in something close to astonishment, for he had never heard such a thing. He had seen young people before who wanted to leave home, or who wanted to travel in his company to a distant town and then leave him, or who wanted to escape a cruel stepfather who would follow them and make trouble for the circus. But they had all demanded a sum of money for their services and were quick to steal his money and slip away unannounced.

"You will not steal?"

"I will not steal; on my honor."

"You will not lie to me?"

"I will not lie to you; on my honor."

"And you will do everything I tell you to?"

"I will do everything you tell me to just as long as I can return here in a year and a day and you will not stop me; on my honor."

The wages were quite satisfactory to the master of the circus and the intensity of the boy gave the master a sense of security in granting the request. "Yes, you may join us for the year and a day when we shall once more be outside the walls of this abbey. But I warn you, that if you are trying to fool me..."

he look of distress on the boy's face told the master that he must hold his tongue and to suggest that there was duplicity in the request would have been to defile the honor of St. Genesius. So he stopped in the middle of his warning and repeated, "Yes, you may join us for a year and a day." And the two realized that a commitment had been made on both sides from which there was no return or possibility of dissembling. Without another word, the boy walked over to the dancing bear. He picked up an armful of straw and began to clean the bear's cage. The master of the circus followed him with his eyes, seemed satisfied, and went over to the jugglers to check on the coins that had been thrown to them.

On the last day of the festival, there was the usual mixture of last minute bartering and performing. What had not yet been sold or traded was now seen in a different light and the loving treasures of yesterday now took on the cast of objects to be bought and sold. Those who had done well this year were already packing up their goods and already saying farewell to their friends whom they would not see again for a year. The whole frenzy of setting up booths was reversed and the flags and streaming colors were carefully folded into neat little bundles and tied with the same string that had held them together over the years.

The thrill of having made a particularly shrewd bargain mixed with the zest of collecting last minute memories against next winter's long nights and tales for the telling and retelling were hoarded for careful distribution against an evening's monotony. It was all they could have desired and more; it was all they had anticipated and more; it was all their dreams at once and more. It was the end of the fair and now it was time to go home.

I have not told you the boy's name until now because I wanted you to know him before you knew what to call him. His name was Martin: a good, strong saint's name given him by his mother who was barely a wife before she became a widow. He was raised in the village of — well, that part does not matter. Let us just say that he was raised among simple loving folk by his mother, who prized him above all else in the world. For he was all she really had in the world. She had married a soldier who once passed through their village, but mind you, he was no ordinary soldier. His mother often told him how handsome her husband had been, how strong, how tender. She told him how his army had marched through the village on the way to one of their usual wars but how unusual he had been. He did not order the peasants about nor did he demand their bread or their chickens as had the others. He had come gently to her door and had asked quietly for something to eat and he had paid her handsomely for the simple crust she gave him from his meager soldier's pay. While he was in the room, she felt the room grow smaller and her breath came in short gasps as though she were suddenly thrust on a mountain peak from which she wished never to descend.

As he was packing his soldier's gear, word came to the village that the fighting had moved on but no one knew where. The sound of cannon could be heard rumbling down some distant mountain, like a spring avalanche portending possible death or disaster. Sometimes a single soldier would be seen. His pack hastily thrown on his back and in his eyes was the haunted look of the deserter. But no one knew just where the army was and, rather than have the forces rush off to an abandoned field of combat, the order came that the soldiers in the village were to stay where they were until further notice. So our gentle soldier remained in the house, really a hut, of the maiden. The second day rolled into the third, the third into a week, and the week into a fortnight.

Their courtship was as honest as it was brief. Both knew they did not have time for the rituals of romance or coquetry. The parish priest, knowledgeable in the ways of love and of war, was pleased to perform the simple ceremony which made one of the two. But three days later, a harried messenger rode into the village, his uniform splattered with mud and blood, his horse white with the froth of haste and emergency. The soldiers were ordered to the front which was now two mountain ranges away. The bridegroom kissed his wife who stood numb with the shock that the inevitable was upon them. "I love you and I will return for you. But if I should die and it should be God's will that we have a child, know that I will spend my heaven watching over both of you and protecting you." And then he joined the forces meeting at the edge of the village, became one of their number, and marched off with his heart heavy and his determination strong.

The bride watched as the soldiers became smaller and smaller, marching out to relieve their embattled army. Her determination was no less strong nor her heart less heavy. He will return, she promised herself, but if he should die and if God should grant us child, I will name the child Martin after his father.

The gentle soldier's army was routed, two mountain ranges away, and the enemy came down the path the soldiers had taken. They stormed into the village, burned houses, killed the villagers, slaughtered the cattle and the sheep, and then moved on like the implacable torrent of a mountain stream. The bride came out of hiding and then ran to the field, two mountain ranges away, to look for her husband. She rushed to the wounded, those leaning against trees for support and those lying on the ground, too weak to seek that support. The groans made a constant wail in the wind and it seemed that all the misery in the world had coalesced into this one dull sound of pain and defeat. But Martin was not there.

hen she went to the dead and searched for his body. Hers it was to turn over a body and look into the face of death and see that more than humanity was wounded in this battle. But Martin was not among the dead.

he returned to the wounded and asked if any knew of her beloved and the answer was always the same, "I did not see him." But from one she learned that he had been the hero of the futile field, if such fields can ever breed heroes. He had fought with the strength of ten and had rescued scores from the jaws of certain death by his valor but no, I do not know what happened to him. From another she learned that he had put himself between death and his companions and had been a very David in the presence of Saul but no, I do not know what happened to him.

As the dark approached, she gathered firewood for the wounded and made bandages of strips of soldier clothing. To all the question was the same as their wounds were tended, "Have you seen Martin? Which way did he go?" And always the answer was the same, "No, I do not know what happened to him."

Heartsick and weary, she returned to her burned hut, the scene of such recent bliss and love. In the ashes she sat waiting, hoping that he had escaped, praying that he would come. In the light of dawn she sat, and watched, and hoped, and prayed. All through the day, she waited. Just before noon she again returned to the battlefield, two mountain ranges away. Again she looked among the dead and the wounded. Again and again she asked her question, "Have you seen my Martin?" And again and again the litany of denial pounded in her ears.

We need not dwell on the next desperate weeks and months. She continued to return, hoping that Martin had been lost in the surrounding hills or had been somehow separated. She waited even past the time that her condition began to show and it was obvious to those who still lived that the cycle of life would continue even in this arena of death. When her time came, she brought forth a man child and he was given the name Martin.

And we need not dwell either on the next several years, years spent in watching for the missing soldier and working to make a home for young Martin. The boy grew, a beautiful boy really. He possessed his mother's beauty, but in its masculine expression. And he possessed his father's gentleness and strength. Virtue rested upon him as easily as mist on a mountain peak.

He did not fight with the other boys in his village, not because he could not but because he would not. And the other boys were somehow respectful, although they themselves would push and tease each other. But when it came to Martin, they knew that an aura of protection surrounded him and they felt foolish when they tried to test his limits. But in all other things he was as playful, as mischievous, as daring, and as bold as they.

One day, when Martin was just growing into manhood, he came home to find his mother sick in bed. She tried to get up and prepare his dinner, but her legs would not hold her and she fell back upon the bed, weak and exhausted. The love between them was so strong that neither had to mention the obvious. She had no last advice to impart and no last request to invoke. Both knew that the dying woman longed to join her husband in the realm beyond the

41

mountain ranges, even beyond the sea, and even yet beyond the stars. Her leave taking was as simple as their lives had been and no regret marred the dignity of her death. "I lost one Martin to war," she said. "May I lose the second one to peace." Those were her last words, and they were said with her last breath.

Martin buried his mother as his last act in that village. He picked up his few possessions, mostly small mementos of his simple life, put them in his sack and departed the village without once turning back. "What is important to me," he said, "is not in the village but in my heart."

You already know of the trades that Martin practiced, of the fields that he tended, of the animals he cared for. We need not follow him through each step of his apprenticeship, at least until just before he presented himself to the Abbot. One night, when there was no moon and the stars were almost blinding in their closeness, he felt a disturbance in his soul. He looked into the night and saw blackness behind blackness. It was not fear he felt but a sense of need to get beyond the stars, beyond his talents, an urgency to follow a voice he could not hear.

This is not enough, he thought. I must do and be more. I want to serve God. Having come to that realization, there was nothing more for him to consider. In the first morning light, he again picked up his sack and sought the Abbot on the feast of St. Genesius. What happened at the fair and of his conversation with Father Abbot you also know, so we now can return to the disappointed Martin as he helps the troupe of players pack their clubs and store their banners and prepare the cages for the show they will present in the South before the severity of Lenten prohibition spreads its demands over laughter and gaiety.

And Lent for Martin could not have been more austere had he been the monk he desired to be. His disappointment was so numbingly acute that he could not begin in earnest his service of God. He felt that the Abbot did not understand the seriousness of his request or worse ,that he had been at fault in not explaining it better. He took the Abbot's words to come back in a year and a day as a judgment on his unworthiness and for the first time, he actually did see himself as unworthy. God had given him a father he never knew and had taken his mother away. Maybe those were ways that God was punishing him for being unworthy to serve him and the Abbot saw this. Maybe that was why he must perform this penance.

IV.

The Abbot watched as Martin walked dejectedly from the Abbey. Had the lad known it, the pain of separation was far greater to the older man than to the younger. The Abbot watched until the sight of the leather jerkin was lost in the crowd and the noise of the fair had enfolded the boy in its embrace.

Sadly, with a weight he did not know if he could bear, the Abbot closed the heavy abbey door behind him and found himself in the empty abbey church. He slowly walked down the long nave, looking all the time at the high altar as though hoping to find there something which his heart sought. How often he had come to this refuge and how often he had found answers to the questions that tormented him. He had come when he too, as a novice, had requested admission to the abbey. Like a squire on the verge of knighthood, he had knelt all night long in the darkened church and prayed that he would be accepted into the only company of brothers he knew who worked so diligently for peace.

He had come again for the vigil before pronouncing his vows, which closed his former life to him and opened up his future of chosen obscurity. He came when he heard that the monks were considering making him their new abbot. And how often he had kept silent vigil ever since. When questions of import came to him, or when there were decisions which called for wisdom mingled with mercy, or when the conduct of the monks needed reprimand mixed with understanding, or when his past returned to him in unexpected glimpses of memory, he would repair to the abbey church and pour out his soul to his God and there he found courage, or wisdom, or compassion. So it was instinctive with him that he should now stand before the altar and pray for the young man he had just sent away.

I have already told you that young Martin was like a mountain climber who finds his moment of integrity ahead of him. He is the continual quester; the restless soul who knows no surcease from his quest. And the Abbot, I have said, is the fisher of pearls who knows that he has seen the one great pearl in all the seas and who finds his soul restless until he can grasp that pearl once more in his hands. He knows that it will never be and yet is never discouraged by that knowledge. That once he saw it is sufficient. For him, like Elijah, the strength of that food would sustain him for the rest of his journey, however long it may be or however arduous it may become.

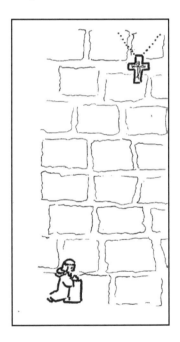

The Abbot, with automatic habit, slipped into the choir stall and sank to his knees. His gaze was fixed on the flickering red candle light which shone near the tabernacle. His mind was as empty as his heart was full. No words rose to his lips, and no plans, no ideas crowded his thoughts. It was as though the whole of the universe had coalesced in the candlelight and the eyes which saw it. Occasionally, tears formed in the bottom of his eyelids, but no tears fell on his cheeks. That single glimmer of light held him in its thrall, would not let him go, but also spoke to him in the language that is beyond the words of men.

The Abbot heard the abbey bell announce to the monks that it was time for Matins and he heard, faintly on the edge of his consciousness, the rustle of robes as the monks gathered to give praise to God in the first watch of the night.

As the first strains of the chant ascended into the darkened vaults of the church the Abbot, with an effort that faithfully reflected his military background, left the place his soul had visited and looked at his surroundings. As he limned each monk's face in his mind, he knew that he had chosen wisely in sending young Martin forth for the year and a day. He knew that innocence cannot be bought at the cost of inexperience and that dedication cannot be purchased with mere determination. It is the gift which costs most dearly that is the most treasured in the giving. And it is only when we know the value of the gift we give that we can be truly generous, just as receiving requires more of charity and generosity than giving. If our gifts are viewed as mere straw, of what value is the gift? But his knowledge gave him scant comfort and his sense of loss was no less acute.

For I must tell you now that young Martin was the Abbot's son. Abbot Martin, for we must give him now his proper name, had recognized the lad immediately at the fair. He saw the boy's mother, not only in the features, but in the stance, the demeanor, the carriage, the tilt of the head, the ingenuousness of the eyes. Had young Martin been taller or shorter, deformed or ugly, had he been badly scared or a cripple, still would the Abbot have known him.

Had he worn rags and walked with the beggars, or had he come carried high on a royal chair, still he would have known his son.

In remembering the young man's face, the Abbot saw the battlefield from which he had been carried; he saw the time he had spent as a slave in a foreign land, his escape, his frantic search for his wife and child. In an instant, he relived his years of wandering and then, like the roll of thunder that echoes through a mountain pass, he heard the thunder mingle with the voices of the monks at their prayers:

To you our praise is due in Zion, O God,
To you we pay our vows, you who hear our prayer.
To you all flesh will come with its burden of sin.
Too heavy for us, our offenses, but you wipe them away.
Blessed are those whom you choose and call,
To dwell in your courts.
We are filled with the blessings of your house,
Of your holy temple.

With each measured cadence, the Abbot found strength returning to him. He had not realized how drained he had become. And with the bodily strength came spiritual renewal and although still elusive: peace, the kind of peace which can come only after the temptation to despair has been successfully repulsed and the sense of hope mitigated by the sense of loss.

Surely, every man wants to be considered a patient man. For impatience seems to indicate a weakness, a flaw that must be eliminated— even perhaps, a sin that must be confessed. Therefore any show of impatience, any indication that perfect peace does not rule the heart is kept hidden. And that is a shame, for impatience is really the virtue which keeps hope alive. Because of our impatience, we live on the level of our dream at the same time we pay attention to the world around us. It is impatience which gives us courage in the face of suspicion and the danger of being misunderstood. It is impatience which challenges us to transform our dreams into the already present future.

Abbot Martin could not hide his impatience from his monks nor from himself. He tried to tell himself that God's will cannot be forced, nor can it be presumed. We have not been made God's counselors and were not present when the heavens were formed and the mountains fashioned and brought forth. Still, if the Abbot had not allowed himself his impatience, he would have found himself faced with a despair which bordered on terror. Never once in the entire year had he considered the possibility that his son would not return. That was a thought which could not be entertained. That, to him, was the sin not his anticipation of the boy's arrival.

The next year for Abbot Martin was one filled with indescribable expectation. Lent came with its penances and vigils, and then Lent gave way to the Resurrection of Christ and of the spring. Summer's heat burned no less searingly than the anticipation which burned in his heart. The harvest in the fields was no less bountiful than the Advent prayers the Abbot garnered for presentation to the Child Jesus to be offered at the crib. With the spring and the fruitfulness of the earth came the premonitions of life and the fulfillment of hope, for Abbot Martin was not given to wishing. For him, a wish was a dream that belittled the wisher. But hope was the firm realization that the not-yet would soon be.

He counted his days, not by the pages of the breviary which told of the saints and their celebrations, but by the shortening and then the lengthening of the light. Not one of the monks suspected what went on in their Abbot's heart, for he was disciplined: first to his military service and then to his monastic vows. His duty to the monks was clear and he never once flagged in the exercise of that duty. But within him, he found that he would recite over and over to himself, "My son, my son."

And so it was that the festival time once again approached. He felt the thrill in the air which portends the arrival of the fair. He could sense the tightening of the very air which would announce that Lent would once more be upon them. He watched from his window as the first of the villagers came to stake out a favorite site. There was still an occasional patch of snow on the leeward side of the abbey as the area for the booths was measured off, carefully and indeed, lovingly.

The circus jugglers came with their noise and their colors and quickly set up their booth. The bear was still there, and the trained dogs and the performers. But of young Martin, there was nothing. All the other tents were quickly in place and the chaos of the preparation gave way to the frenzy of the fair. At last, old Brother Guillam, another year telling on his weathered face, came once more to escort the Abbot through the passage and stairway to the fair for the opening blessing.

The Abbot's eyes searched everywhere for young Martin. He did not curtail his appointed task nor cut short the usual blessing or a word of comfort to those who looked on him with such trust and devotion. With an effort which cost him dearly, he restrained his impulse to run to the circus performers and ask for the lad. In due course, with nothing to betray his interest, he walked to the place of the performers and asked in a voice which he did not recognize. "And where is the lad I sent off with you last year? I expected to see him with you."

The leader of the circus looked away with an embarrassment which frightened the Abbot. "We had some trouble crossing a swollen river. I lost two horses and one full wagon of costumes. Martin tried to save them and was lost when a log, floating from up the river, grazed his head. That much I saw. But after that, I did not see Martin again. I am sorry, Father Abbot, I tried to reach him, but the waters were too swift. Nor did we find the body, although we looked downstream. It was in autumn that this happened, and the rains in the Carpathian Mountains were severe. There was nothing I could do. I am sorry, Father Abbott," he repeated, "There was nothing I could do."

Now there is a dying beyond death which is reserved by the good God for those who would put themselves in His hands. For it is not the moment after death which we fear, for then we know that we will rest lightly and warmly in His hands. It is the actual moment of death which distresses us when all of our days will be totaled and the account of stewardship given. And there is the moment just before death when the heart freezes in its course and the body goes numb, not with fear and dread but with an intense expectation that borders on complete suspension of all sensation and yet all sensations are one.

It was just that moment which the Abbot felt upon hearing of his son's death. He could not react and he could not withdraw. He was caught in the underwater world of all lost pearls without light or darkness, without shape or form. He made the sign of the cross over the circus performers but he had no voice with which to utter the blessing.

Abbot Martin would not allow himself to be deterred from his usual routine. He watched himself as though it were a stranger to his body move from group to group. He saw a face smile at the people but he could not relate that smile to his own face. He watched another Abbot tend the monks as they prepared themselves for their part in the festivities, their helping of the farmers unload their cheeses and artifacts, offering an extra hand when the tents were too heavy for their users. The younger monks were as noisy as they were occasionally useless. But that too was part of the festival and the Abbot would not interfere with the ritual of the fair. But still, it was like watching another Abbot, another man, oversee and take pleasure in the feast he could never taste again. His heart was heavy with the news that he could not, would not, accept. If his son had been dead, he would have known it. His heart would not have lied to him nor would his God have imbued his soul with such hope if that hope were only to be dashed. God did not bring him his son only to separate them again. The news did not deflect his watch, but made him realize that his watch must take on a different form.

Again the alien Abbot noticed everything and yet saw nothing. He walked from booth to booth, gave his smile and encouragement to each one, and when the other Abbot found a voice, pronounced that in this year of Our Lord, God's blessings had again been abundant. But in all of this ritual, the soul of the Abbot Martin of the lost son was numb.

"My son, my son," he heard with the ears of his heart, repeated over and over. "Would that I had died instead of you."

Now there are times when we simply cannot act and our habits must do our acting for us. Just such a time was this for Abbot Martin. It was as though he was standing beside himself, watching this other, this stranger, perform acts and deeds, say things and respond to questions, smile. It is like the diver of pearls who, from his underwater world, sees the boat above him and sees faces distorted by

the ripples and waves on the surface of the sea. They —
and he — are there, and yet they are not there. They move
in different worlds and still are visible but unknown,
uncommunicative to each other.

The first day of the fair had held no further surprises,
nor did the second. And now, on the third and last day, the
numbness began to leave the Abbot and with the loss of
numbness came the presence of pain which made all his
battle wounds mere scratches on a child's knee. For with
the pain came an uneasiness about the Abbot which only
the most discerning would detect. He was impelled by a
force he could neither understand nor control to watch the
gate. And as he watched, it was a though the emptiness of
the gate grew, expanding and engulfing the gathering stars.
He felt himself pulled into that blackness and become one
with it. For the numbness had gone through the pain and
was entering into another realm of existence, an existence
not ordinarily given to mortals to experience or to share.
There, in that domain beyond knowledge and
understanding, is the kingdom of truth and conviction.

As the campfires around the few remaining wagons
grew lower and then diminished into a gentle glow, and the
moon-free stars covered the sleepers with their blanket of
gracious care, Abbot Martin became restless and uneasy in
his cell. The exhaustion of the last three days, instead of
offering him slumber as surcease from his agony, now
sharpened his perceptions. On the edges of his mind he
could hear the whisper of his name: "Martin. Martin."

He rose from his cot, walked through the corridors of
the abbey, through the vastness of the abbey church, and
out into the beckoning darkness. The whisper grew louder
as he made his way through the still smoldering embers of
the campfires and through the gate. Here the whisper was
louder, more assured, and totally compelling. Even had the
Abbot known that he would walk past the edge of the world
and beyond the rim of the universe of stars, he also knew

he could not pause nor fail to take that next inexorable, predestined step.

And then he saw him, sitting under the huge oak tree that formed one of the boundaries of the monastery lands. It was not so much that he was seen, for no matter how brilliant the stars, nothing was clear in the shadow of the tree. It was that the blackness had an outline, a coalescence of night itself, huddled at the foot of the tree. And as the heart and only the heart, knows the difference between the friend who comes at midnight and the thief, the Abbot knew his son had returned. He walked to the tree, looked down at his son, and said, "My son, you have returned."

The boy was not surprised to see the Abbot. Indeed, it was as though he expected they would meet, here on this tenebrous plain as two old friends, both aware of the other's habits. But young Martin could barely move. His hair was matted with tangles and dried blood, and his face was like an icon set in a dark frame. The tatters of his clothes lay about him, now useless against the evening chill. Yet even in his wasted condition, he had a dignity about him and a fierce determination in his eyes that seemed to proclaim, 'See? I told you I would return in a year and a day, my purpose completed.'

Whether it was his return from the quest or the quest itself, which brought him to this condition was irrelevant, and both Martins knew it. It was evident to both that

53

whatever strength the lad had possessed had been spent in coming to this place on this day. There was a slight sadness but no regret in young Martin's voice as he said, "I'm sorry Father Abbot, but I cannot ask to enter your monastery."

The Abbot knelt down beside the boy and took him in his arms. For the space of time that it takes for the Big Dipper to descend and Orion to grow pale, Martin held his son against him and the two spoke through their love that knows no language and which no verbal exchange can validate.

As the lark heralded the arrival of the Morning Star, the boy looked into the Abbot's face and asked, "Father Abbot, do you remember the question you asked me one year and a day ago?"

"Yes, I remember."

"I told you I saw colors, and shapes, banners and wagons, children and old people."

"I remember very well, my son." The Abbot's voice was barely audible through his constricted throat. His breath was shallow and irregular as his vision blurred with stinging tears.

"Now please, Father Abbot. Ask me again."

"My son," the Abbot began. He inhaled as deeply as his wrenching emotion would permit. Then in one heroic effort he said again, "My son, now what do you see?"

The boy's face became radiant in the light of the listening stars which paused in their diamond brilliance to hear their names called, each by each. A smile of fathomless unbounded peace spread across his face. "I see... I see... I see them all and so much more. Ah, such beauty. And I see..." His last word was lost in the gentle wind that caressed the protecting oak. "I see...," The voice and the wind blended into one gracious whisper and medley of union. Then, just as gently, they ceased.

Young Martin in his father's arms became light as air and elusive as dreams. With the answer still on his pale lips, he followed his thought into the realm of unending peace.

The Abbot held his son in his arms, knowing that the mountain climber had reached his peak. There in the first rays of dawn, darkness loosened its grip on night, on doubt, even on the quest and embraced the boy in their golden glow. The stars withdrew in humility and awe from the sight and returned to their resting place beyond the sun.

V.

My tale has now come to its end. I told you there was no moral except perhaps, for me. For I am the Abbot Martin and I have told you how I lost then found and again lost my son. But as I lost my wife, I gained my son. And when I lost my son, I gained my God. The pearls that slipped through my fingers were lovely. They were precious and I would not trade one of them though they have cost me dearly.

And now I am an old man, a teller of tales to the young. Occasionally the armies march past our monastery in their never-ending search for the meaning of their lives. We have seen heroes and cowards and we know that you and I are no different than they. Our battles may be waged in darkness or in light and our victories may be indistinguishable from our defeats. They may be fought on the plain beyond the two mountain ranges or they may be fought in the recesses of our own hearts. But each struggle carries within itself the seeds of its own outcome and — eventually — its own peace.

A Simple Tale

They don't come here very often anymore. Sure they do sometimes, but not often. And then it's usually because it's an anniversary, or it's Memorial Day, or it's Mother's Day, or an excuse to go for a Sunday ride for old time's sake. It's not that they don't care. It's just that there are so many other things to do, and so many other places to go to, and so many ways to forget that this place is here at all.

And look, you can see it's really nice here too. That's part of the shame. Quiet. Peaceful. Like the way it was supposed to be when the Almighty invented death. The markers don't count for too much. Look at the way they're all fading. Strange to think of stone fading, but just look at them. Can't even read some of them. It's all part of a family plot, but whose? Maybe there's a record somewhere. But maybe there shouldn't be one either. The only record that counts is in the bones underneath that get smaller and smaller each year. And a lot of them who couldn't abide each other on this side find they're all clumped together laying side by side for eternity. . Like they chose their hereafter while they were still here and got a chance to watch it happen.

The markers are like mirrors that show back the face of the living who picked them. What they didn't do in passing, they do forever when the passing would have been better. Maybe the daily part was too hard to do and the staying part was for others to get a good look at. The dying is always private, but the show for the dead is permanent.

Maybe the stones on top are just keeping up with what going on below. Ever think of that?

And look out there, beyond that hill. That's where the town used to be. From here you never saw the houses, like the two places were kept separate and had nothing to do with each other. It was a nice little town too. The folks were always at war with themselves, deciding if the houses were for themselves or for their grandchildren too. Some thought of the land they were building on and some thought just of the job they were doing in the hills, a place to stay until the hill was all dug out.

It was a grand little town and I wish you could have seen it when the folks here were up and walking. It wasn't like the town was thought of before it was here. The ore came first, then the folks, and then the town. It was the men first, then the women, and then came the children.

When the right time came for the men or the women or the children, there'd be a regular procession with singing and crying when they brought up a new one. And it wasn't just the town that was all caught up in the proceedings. It was everything. Even the air was waiting for something to happen in it. The un-sound covered the hill as though the shroud of the dead could reach right up here through the sky and hug everything.

Even the birds knew. Out of reverence or fear — who knows? — they held their feeding and mating sounds in their throats, waiting for something they couldn't see or eat. But maybe they heard the sadness growing out of the town and knew their place in the sorrow, and they knew the place of their silence in the ritual.

58

You could hear them before you saw them. And the singing was always real pretty. The top voices came in clear on a spring morning, more like an echo of a breeze or a feeling in the ear that you know should be there but maybe isn't quite heard yet. And then pretty soon it would be the lower sounds, part human and part like a floor you can stand on. Singing about the gentle hands of Jesus, or about shepherds and sheep and angels. And there was always a kind of not-quite-heard wail under that. It wasn't just like sadness in sound. It was more like not liking what they were doing and being somehow sorrier for themselves for doing it than they thought they ought to be. But it was pretty because you didn't hear it at any other time.

The saddest of all were the young, either being carried or walking along side. You'd know that there'd be a bunch of other little ones hanging on to bigger hands, being dragged along with no idea what was going on, just being scared. Sometimes, though, they knew better than the big ones. It was probably because there was so little to remember of the little ones and so little for the little ones to take with them to the other side.

So the sound would get louder and louder even before the first of the people could be seen. It was just this side of wailing and that side of church singing, like about five notes playing at the same time but all on the same word. But you couldn't make out the word: you'd just know it was there, waiting for the next word to push it on. The words got pulled in one by one until they made a procession all by themselves.

They'd walk of course. Mr. Scripps the undertaker would always lead, as if they wouldn't know where to go if he didn't show them. The top of his tall hat was a light for the folks to follow and they felt terrible things would happen to them if they didn't follow at the pace he set. And then under the hat you'd see his face, long and lean, and kind of leathery, like he was born in the sun at age

59

sixty-five, all wrinkly, and time neither added wrinkles or absolved them since. It was a solemn face, with just the right amount of authority with a no-nonsense look mixed in. His eyes had a distance to them, but also a softness which let you know that he now knew all the secrets of the dead, but he wasn't going to tell no one. It was comforting somehow. The people knew they could follow him easy and they weren't going to get lost or go to the wrong grave, although there was always only the one open and no one was going to get lost going there. Under the hat was the face, and under the face was the body that held it all up. It too was long and lean, dressed always in black for there is no other color to respect the dead but black. Erect, like a judge just about to pass a harsh but just sentence everyone knew was coming. Like there were no more surprises or expectations or waiting for something. He was a rock you could rest against, not really friendly, but no real enemy neither.

From where we're standing he would look like he was rising, no effort at all, out of a pit you couldn't quite see. There was no swaying or movement, but a kind of floating that didn't depend on the body. And the singing would get louder and louder and then you could hear the words real clear as the people following also rose up out of that invisible place.

The box would be mostly hidden from sight by the bodies of the bearers. You'd get only a quick peek at it as the men, looking more solemn than they really felt, puffed from the effort of carrying that awkward contraption up the hill. They'd look strained and uneasy, wearing clothes they forgot they had and wouldn't wear again until the next funeral which maybe would be their own. You could see they were thinking about that too, the way they looked around them, saw their own kin's place and real deliberate looked somewhere else. They knew where their future was but they didn't want too much future right now.

There'd always be flowers on the casket. And they were real pretty too. Flowers from around the house of the dead one usually. Jonquils, and violets, and sometimes lilacs and forsythia, but the time for lilacs and forsythia was always short. Chrysanthemums grow pretty good here and you can usually count on some of them. When they came here in winter, there may be some made-flowers with colors too bright to be real. Folks thought of the thought of them more than of the look of them. And it was always appreciated.

Behind the casket bearers would come the family, a husband or wife first hanging on the arms of their closest, and children if they were grown or brothers or other male kin. The men who were used to giving the orders and commanding the ship of the family seemed somehow lost and a little pathetic. The storm of unaccustomed grief kept them off balance and confused them as they held onto their right of taking charge. They hoped this too would be like a barn raising, or a cow calving, or ore digging, and they didn't know what to do with the difference. But they were mostly more unknowing than the women folk who stayed pretty close to the background. And these moments really belonged to the women folk. They were born knowing how to deal with the heavy parts of birth and death, even if they didn't always know how to handle the getting from the one to the other all the time. But they'd all come in a line, like they had to put their footprints just so or they'd have to start all over again, and go back to a place they wouldn't recognize when they got there.

They'd all come too. Missing a burial was not something you could do. You'd be more missed for not being there than if you'd hung out a sign saying you'd got no time for funerals. Folks notice who isn't there and quickly forget who is. Ever notice that? It's like on this side of the grave where you regret the things you didn't do more than be sorry for the things you actually did.

So they'd all be there, wearing just the right kind of face and keeping pace with Mr. Scripps, all hobbled together somehow and couldn't move without his say-so.

And he'd lead the whole shebang right up to the grave I'd dug the night before. And then he'd stop, like he was either inspecting it or doing honor to the pit, checking to see if it was wide enough or deep enough, if the sides were straight enough and the boards across it strong enough. Behind him, everybody just stopped right there, holding their breaths, looking at his tall hat or the back of his head. The moment of judgment. Either the dead would have to go back to the living or could get on with the business of being dead, depending on Mr. Scripps' decision about the grave.

But he'd always give his silent permission so the folks could breathe easy again and keep going on with their business by giving the open ground a tiny nod, moving to the far side, raising his hands out level and draw the casket bearers forward. It was Moses doing the Red Sea opening, and it did set the folks in motion again. Everyone knew the judgment had been made and that the reward of the dead could be granted.

The bearers moved to either side of the grave, struggling not to fall in, facing each other on either side, stood up artificial straight and waited for instructions on what to do next, no matter how often they'd done it. And with a nod from Mr. Scripps, they'd stand back and then move up to where he was standing. You could see they were real glad to have this part over with because by now the clothes were beginning to have an effect on them, like someone who wakes up in the morning and finds out he's put on the wrong skin.

Slowly, even more slowly than they'd come up the hill, the folk gathered around the grave, shoulder to shoulder, working out their own order of right to grieve in front of the townspeople. Everyone's head was bowed, taking little peeks out of the sides of their eyes to make sure the bow was low enough. It would have been bad business to be seen to grieve more than the family did. Miz Harris did that one time and they never really forgave her.

There was always a parson or a minister or a priest there, even for the tramps that crawled into town just in time to die. The folks wouldn't have stood for a burial any more than they would a baby without the benefit of clergy. Next to Mr. Scripps, the minister was the most important person there, even more important than the husband or wife. Maybe even more than the dead. He was the one who let it be known that we could now commend the soul to the Almighty and not worry about it too much anymore. He was the one who gave the dead permission to get on with whatever they had to be about now. We knew we would have to answer to Mr. Scripps if we got something wrong, but we would have to answer to the clergy if damnation happened for something we didn't do.

Except for Deacon Hanson being sober, you never noticed who the parson was. It was like a talking photograph that belonged on the wall of the best parlor and could be taken down on occasions of family reunions for purposes of identifying who the others in the picture were. But they didn't seem to mind, and why should they? They got to use the Bibles and flip through pages that were already memorized from the other funerals they had done. They didn't have to say anything comforting, or condemning, or sad, or judging. They just had to make the right sounds and make them sound right. It was always the doing of it that mattered, not what was done.

So the words would be said and pronounced slow and solemn to the tops of heads, bowed in various degrees of bowing. Long sighs would mix with the words like 'resurrection and the life,' 'immortal soul,' 'forgiveness of sin,' 'on the last day.' And the folks would stay huddled together around the grave like rabbits in a thunder storm, knowing what their next move would be but not wanting to be the first to make it. So there was always a space of silence in which everyone got restless. The closest to the dead would sneak a look at the parson to see if there was anything more coming, and when there wasn't they'd raise their heads full up and put on their bravest faces. That was the signal for the others to stand up too, take a big breath and give vent to their restlessness. No more to do here, they'd seem to say. Nothing added and nothing left out. Just like it's supposed to be and a quick nod of gratitude that they weren't going to be the one being left behind. They always found comfort in that. Besides, they'd been gone from their homes long enough.

Then Mr. Scripps would raise his head the highest and clear his throat. That 'harrumph' was the signal for everyone to really relax and get ready for their going back down the hill. "In the name of the bereaved, I want to thank you all for coming this morning." And then there would be a real long pause, long enough for each one to catch the gratitude that had come his or her way. And then he would add, "We may now bury the deceased."

That was the signal for the last act of the ritual, the moment everyone dreaded coming but wanted over with real quick. The bearers would raise one side of the casket, take out the boards that were holding it up, slip a rope under it, and then lower the box. They always tried to do it nice and level, but it was always like a see-sawing. As they lowered the box down, you could be real glad the dead were dead or they'd be seasick by the time they got to the bottom. Then they wiggled the rope free and stood back.

First the family walked up, that was their right and they held onto it jealously. They took a handful of dirt and tossed it on the casket. And then they'd stand alongside the grave and wait for the others to seal the ritual. Dirt falling on the casket was like no other sound on earth. It was an awful sound, like a thump that thumped in your soul and found you empty. The final trumpet would have no more lonely sound or set up more lonely feelings than that thump of dirt on the casket. It was final proof that their business was done here and that they should go now and best not look back.

And that's just what they did. A line was quickly made up and everyone took a handful of dirt and tossed it in. Some folks took longer than others. And some didn't hardly look where they were tossing the dirt. They'd just toss and keep walking. But after the throwing of the dirt, they just kept walking, joining family and friends, walking lighter and easier the farther they got from the grave.

And then it was the family's turn. You always expected them to take the longest and they did. It was their right and they hung onto it. Sometimes there would be a waving of handkerchiefs and shoulders shaking and long looks at the dirt that filled the top of the casket. We all knew they could take as long as they liked as long as they didn't take too long. Most took a special pretty flower to put in the family Bible to be forgotten until it was joined by the next funeral flower.

But then finally, the family too would travel down the hill and know that they were waited for by those now out of sight.

After the last of the townsfolk and family had thrown their handful of dirt in, Mr. Scripps would stand, silent as a statue until the top of the last head had gone below the hill. Then he'd turn and give me a nod, never saying anything since we both knew our business, and he would follow the silence down the hill.

Then I'd lift my shovel. I always kept the shovel hidden or down on the ground so that the seeing of it would not upset the folks. Seems like they could stand almost anything except seeing my shovel. Like nothing was really over until I showed them that it was over and it was a symbol of finality and death, more than the casket, more than the parson's words, more than Mr. Scripps presence even, more even that the thumping of the earth on the casket. There was no reprieve for them if they saw my shovel. And they knew it. And they feared it.

So I'd lift my shovel from off the ground or from where it was leaning against a high tombstone and prove their fears were right. Then I'd look around to make sure there was no one around. There never was, but I'd look anyway. I'd shovel the dirt back from where I'd taken it the night before, pushing it along the side where the thumping of it had not got. And I'd stamp on the loose earth, packing it down as best I could. Then I'd pile some more on, and do some more packing until most of it was used up again. Then I'd pile the rest on so that you could see that there was a new casket under there, making a nice rounded mound. That last part was the hardest, making sure that the mound was even and round. And then I'd take the flowers they'd brought and place them on the mound. The family's flowers always went toward the head, even when they weren't the prettiest. If anyone came, they'd know whose flowers they were and they'd be grateful for that. It didn't cost nothing and folks appreciated it.

If there was some dirt left over, I'd go to the other graves that had sunk with time and spread it out. Somehow it seemed fitting to me that they should share in the bounty that the newly dead couldn't use. I always thought everything should get used and dirt is about the only thing the dead can use anymore.

Well, there's that and the memories.

And the dirt lasts longer.

A Very Good Day

It seems so quiet now, and it is. The sun is just beginning to touch the trees as it slides into the West over the valley. And I will have to go soon and keep up appearances. If I didn't show up, there would be busy little talk and guessing, probably back biting too. So I'll be there, all smiles and joviality. And I'll eat out of the common dish and I'll respond to the proper prayers in the proper way, and then we'll all come back here as we usually do. But it sure won't be quiet then. I have to laugh when I think of that, because I will be the one to get the beehive humming. And don't think it won't be a beehive of angry and stinging bees, looking for someone to vent their anger on. Perhaps it will be more like wasps who need less reason than bees to work themselves into a frenzy. Whatever. It certainly won't be quiet though.

It really was a busy day. And a very productive one at that. While it was still dark, I slipped out of the house where we had been staying for the past three nights, not making a sound. One of the others stirred in his sleep and muttered something just as I was opening the door. I froze in my tracks and waited until I heard him resume his snoring. I don't know which one it was and it really doesn't make any difference. They are all a bunch of toadies and wimps anyway. Not one of them would have the guts to do what I have done. They probably wanted to, but they couldn't bring themselves to it. Instead, they tried to push and shove their insinuations into the conversation or use an opportunity to make their wishes known. But they lacked the guts to face the issue squarely.

Well, I wasn't afraid to and today I took the whole thing into my hands. While all the wimps were sleeping the last peaceful night sleep they would have for a long, long time, I went over and talked to the old men who would be clustered around the temple steps, doing nothing. Sleep is something that escapes the very young and the very old, the young because there is a whole day of adventure ahead, and the old because sleep just doesn't matter anymore. So I knew they would be there, making plans for schemes that would never happen, or preparations for travels they would never make, or rehashing conversations they never had.

It was immediately clear that they had not expected to see me. Surprise, shock, disbelief all sprang to their faces immediately. They hid their reactions just as quickly and tried to pretend that they knew all along that I would show up and they were just puzzled why it should be now. But I know them and their kind. I have seen them far too often with their pretenses and their sham displays of wisdom and knowledge to be taken in by them now. I had come to cut a deal and I know when I have a sucker—or, in this case, suckers—on the hook and I was not going to let them off lightly, you can be sure of that. They were phonies too, pure and simple. I knew it, and they knew that I knew it. It was a game in which we were both masters and would sniff around each other until one of us went in for the kill. And it was a deadly game we were playing too, and one I intended to win.

We began politely enough. The pleasantness of the

spring morning, the crowds in town, the stench of the garbage people were throwing in the streets. You know, all the small questions and answers that mean nothing and aren't intended to. Very gradually we got around to serious matters. Was he still trying to show off? Was he going to come into the temple today and cause more trouble? Did he really think he could get away with humiliating them in front of all those people?

I let them sniff around some more, just waiting for the opportunity to present my plan. But I'm smart enough and patient enough and shrewd enough to let them think it is their plan. Ach! They are so stupid just when they think they are being the most clever. So I shifted the conversation back to the crowds because I knew that would be the sore spot, the way the crowds cheered him and ignored them. They were so greedy for admiration it didn't take much on my part either.

While we were just poking around, the man who would have the final say in any plan came in. He always came late just to show that he was the big boss and top decision maker. As soon as he saw me, he knew that something important was stirring. I liked that. He knew my worth and suspected my purpose just by walking in the door. I could see why he was the decision maker and he had my instant respect. This, I said to myself, is a man of decision. Not a wimp or a dissembler, not someone to say one thing and do another. So all my attention went immediately to him and we had an instant rapport.

"You wish something from us?" He demanded.

"On, the contrary, I am here to offer you something that you wish," I boldly responded.

"What is it that we wish, and what are you suggesting?" He asked without further prelude or introduction. I was taken aback for the moment.

Of course I came to make a suggestion all right, but I did not want to reveal my whole hand too soon. But he demanded too much respect for me just to ignore his directness. So I said, "Well, you have a problem and I just might have the solution."

"And just what is our problem?" He asked and it was more an accusation than a question.

"You are losing the respect of the people, the temple tax isn't paid promptly, the whole place is empty even on the Sabbath so the people can listen to him. I would say that you really do have a problem."

"An annoyance, certainly, and it won't last."

"Perhaps not, but then again it may," I said. "You saw what happened earlier this week. How many came to you later to ask for advice? Or for a teaching? Or an interpretation of a passage in the Torah?" I knew I was scratching a raw nerve and I also knew it was now too late to turn back. "You know what has been happening all over the place these past few years and you know that converts are not coming the way they used to. Two days ago he came in here and threw all the tables around, spilled the money on the floor, let the pigeons fly away and no one stopped him. With all due respect, I would say that you really do have a problem and I repeat, I think I can help you solve it."

We silently stared at each for a moment. Actually, he glared at me. But I knew by his silence that I had hit home, so I stared back and just waited. I became aware of the others because of their silence too. I could see out of the corner of my eye that they were holding their breaths, their eyes were as big as dishes, and they stood motionless as a wall.

"If we have a problem—and, mind you, I'm only saying if—if we have a problem, how do you suggest we solve it?"

"Well," I said and I had been planning this response for weeks now, "well, if he were to be gotten out of circulation for a while. Arrested for disturbing the peace or

for interfering in temple business or for inciting riots—
something like that. You could get the officials to hold him
in jail for awhile and then the people would know just how
powerful he isn't and that he can't even get out of jail." I
could tell this was enticing to him.

"Arrest him," he mused aloud.

"But this is where you will have to be very careful. He
has had a lot of experience in slipping away just when
everyone thought he was caught. Remember the time when
they wanted to make him a king and he seemed to vanish in
the crowd? And remember the time they tried to get him to
stay in town and he just left when no one was looking?
Make no mistake: he is very clever. You can't just arrest
him when his fans are around – and that is where I come
in."

I could see that all this was making an impression on
them all. Getting rid of him and the chance to make a fool
of him at the same time was a temptation that I knew they
would never reject. So I held my tongue and waited.

"Just how would you do this?" The head man asked
after a prolonged silence.

"I could tell you where he will be after supper. It will
be dark. After the full meal, all his followers will be sleepy
and doze off. If you surround the place and come up
quietly, it will all be over in a moment. Before anyone
wakes up in the morning, it will just be another fact that
they will talk about for a bit, get used to, and then move on
to their own business." More silence as the images of
capture and the resulting peace filled their imaginations.

"And what do you get out of this?" The head man
shrewdly asked. I told you he was no dummy but I was
prepared for this too.

"Considering the position you are in, I would think that
you would be properly grateful for an easy solution. It's
not that I want the money, but I do think you should invest
in a concrete way to show your gratitude." Then I waited.

"Since it isn't the money you are interested in, suppose we say ten Roman coins."

"Suppose," I said, "we not waste each other's time. I have what you want and you have what I could use. I think fifty is a nice round number, easy to count, manageable in a single purse. I think fifty might just do it."

"Thirty!" The head man almost shouted and then added, "And it had better be fool proof."

Now thirty was more than I had expected and showed an anxiety I had not fully appreciated. All I had to do was give a time and place and had thought that twenty would be acceptable. And it was at thirty! I felt I should have held out for more, but the deal was struck and that was it. "Oh, it's fool proof indeed. Here is what we can do: I will leave the dinner early on some excuse or another, come here to the temple and meet you and then take you to where he will be after dark. If there are other men around, it might be difficult to recognize him, so I will walk up to him and greet him. As soon as I do that, you will know that you have the right one. Remember what he did before in slipping away. Grab him and hold on. I won't be responsible if he gets away again. Is that understood?"

"It's understood. We will pay you then tonight."

"No, you will pay me now. I told you it was not the money, but I do need some sign of your good faith. The thirty coins would be proof enough."

And so it was done. I still have the coins in my purse, hanging like lead on my belt. The men will all be so absorbed in other things they won't notice that the purse is particularly full. And they are used to sending me out to buy what they need. That's another thing that rankles. We talk about lilies of the field and the poor and giving away anything you can get your hands on, and yet they expect me to buy the provisions, get the lamb at the market, and make sure we have enough eggs. I can't stand their hypocrisy and their disdain for the real world. It's easy enough to preach about another world in another place with other people, and paint beautiful pictures of banquets and fountains. But where are they going to get them if I don't haggle over the prices of the bread and the meat and the wine?

Simon's the worst. He hangs around all the time, pretending to listen to every word and he doesn't understand half of what is being said. He just pretends to so that the master will pay more attention to him. It makes me sick sometimes. He's a large strong man who has fished all his life and is used to hauling in loads of fish. His arms and back are strong. His voice is deep and he could outshout a storm if he had to. And what does he do? He follows around like a puppy, looking for scraps of meat or a scratch behind the ears. He's grown lazy. And even seems proud of it. Well, he's in for a surprise tonight.

Simon isn't the only one who gets my goat. John is always underfoot and the master and he go off on walks together. John always sits close to him at meals and they laugh at jokes that none of the rest of us can hear. Sometimes I think they are talking about me and it makes me furious. I have never been in his confidence and I have never been asked to sit next to him. But when he wants something, who does he send out for it? Me! That's who. John sits and I fetch.

John's brother isn't much better. He hangs around too much to be up to any good. And, boy, do they deserve the mother they got! One time she came crashing in on us when we were in the middle of something important, I forget exactly what, grabbed her sons by the arms and pushed them right in the master's face. "Give them the best places wherever you are going," she demanded. The master almost burst out laughing on that one. The best places, indeed. Here we were, sleeping on the ground, tramping though deserts and hills and she wants them enthroned like royal princes. Well, the little royal princes will have a surprise tonight when they try to bail the master out of jail and have to come to me for the money.

That's where I will come in. Last week I asked the head jailor how much it would cost to get a prisoner out of jail if there were no serious charges against him. "Fifteen coins is the usual gift," he answered. Gift! Right. It would be a bribe, pure and simple. And I loved the irony of what would happen. Here I have thirty coins from the very people who want to put him in jail. I'll come up, give the jailor half, keep the other half, and then the master will praise me for getting him out of a tough spot. Then he will have to pay more attention to me and be grateful for what I have done. I'll have saved his skin and he will then want me to sit next to him at dinner and walk with him as we go from town to town. He'll find out that I can carry on a conversation better than Simon and want me with him when he goes off and leaves the others behind.

I can't see anything wrong with this plan. I'll get the respect I deserve, the master will be grateful, the other men will see that they aren't all that important and that they should have included me more in their plans and conversations. No one loses except the losers. It's beautiful. During the meal I leave, go to the temple, get the guards, come back here to the garden and point out the master. Then maybe he will stop playing games about who is and who is not the messiah. He'll have to take a stand, once and for all. He won't be able to hide behind statements with double meanings. He'll have to act and say I Am or I Am Not and then we can go from there. And I will be the one to force it all into the open.

Yes, this really has been a very good day. Because of me, the whole course of history will take a sharp turn and people for generations will remember me and the courage I showed this very night.

Night. I hadn't realized how dark it was getting and now I have to get back to that upstairs room they have chosen for our supper. Goodness, I hadn't realized how hungry I am.

The Little Donkey

Once upon a time in a far away country, there once lived a beautiful donkey. She was so beautiful that when other donkeys saw her in the field, they would stop and say to themselves, "She is probably the most beautiful donkey I have ever seen. Do you see how gracefully she walks and how prettily she holds her head? She is, indeed, quite the prettiest donkey I have ever seen."

In the neighboring pasture, there lived a handsome young donkey who was strong and gentle, and capable of the most difficult plowing and pulling of carts. He was built like a mighty oak tree that could sway in the wind, but also hold his head against a hurricane and remain standing. Indeed, he was quite the strongest and handsomest donkey anyone had ever seen. Well, one day, on a lovely spring afternoon, when the sun began to stay a little longer in the sky and its warmth began to force the flowers from their sleep, the beautiful girl donkey was walking close to the fence where the handsome young donkey was pulling a heavy load of straw into the barn, and the two of the them saw each other for the first time. The boy donkey stopped in his tracks and could not move, he was so taken up with the girl donkey's beauty. And the girl donkey stopped in the midst of eating fresh grass and saw him looking at her. The two just stood there looking at each other, and they both knew that they would just have to meet and they both knew that they wanted to be friends.

So the two of them trotted over to each other, the girl donkey still chewing grass, and the boy donkey still pulling the straw. The boy donkey said to the girl donkey, "My name is Herman. What's yours?" And the girl donkey said to Herman, "My name is Clara and I am very happy to meet you, Herman."

Now that was how it all began for the two of them. Every day they would trot over to the fence and talk to each other and they talked about everything and nothing, and they laughed with each other and they joked with each other. And pretty soon all of the other donkeys in the two fields knew that Herman and Clara were falling in love and that it wouldn't be long before there would be a wedding in the big barn behind the hill.

And sure enough, the other donkeys were right and Clara and Herman were married in the big barn behind the hill and they kept laughing and joking, and talking about everything and nothing and it wasn't very long when they gave birth to a charming and cute little baby donkey.

Clara said, "We should call her Hermana after you, Herman."

And Herman said, "No, we should call her Clarissa after you, Clara."

And they could not decide on what name to give the baby donkey, so they finally agreed that they would call her Hermana Clarissa Louisa Appleton Marie, or Abbey for short. And that became her name. Little Abbey.

Abbey grew, but not as fast as the other little donkeys and her parents began to fear that she would always be just a little donkey. As Abbey got older she still did not grow very much, but her ears did…and they got bigger and bigger. First they got bigger than her mother's and then they got bigger than her father's and all of the other little donkeys started to laugh at Abbey because her ears were so long.

That wasn't all of it either. Her mouth began to grow and grow. Her face stayed small, but her mouth got bigger and bigger. She could put a whole mouthful of straw into her mouth at one time and then just chew it all day long without having to go back for more. It seemed as if Abbey would not grow up to be strong like her father, nor beautiful like her mother. Sometimes, when Abbey went to bed, she would cry herself to sleep because of all the mean things the other donkeys said about her during the day. And when she prayed, she prayed that her ears and mouth would get smaller so that the other donkeys would not laugh at her.

Now because Abbey's ears were so large, she could hear sounds that other donkeys could not hear. Not even the dogs at the farm or the birds in the trees could hear as well as Abbey. She could hear a wolf coming for the sheep even before the sheep knew of it. She could hear stars speaking to each other and no other donkey had ever been able to do that. She could hear the sun stretching before it go up in the morning and that, of course, was quite unheard of. And so the other donkeys made fun of that too. They said that she was making up stories just because they could not hear these things. And they said she was just trying to get attention from the other donkeys because she was really just an ugly donkey.

So Abbey continued to cry herself to sleep at night and pray that her ears would get smaller and that her mouth would not be so big.

Now all of this went on for some time when a very strange thing happened. One day the wind began to blow out of the north and in the wind there was the promise of snow. As the day grew older, the wind got stronger and stronger and the first flakes of snow began to fall. First they were small flakes, but then they got bigger as the wind got stronger. The wind howled around them so that no one could hear each other speak. And then the snow came so heavily that no one could see the ground in front of them. Abbey was standing between her mother and father because she was so small that they were afraid she would get blown away. And the wind kept getting stronger and blowing harder and Herman and Clara and Abbey huddled together so closely that Abbey could hardly breathe.

The only thing that Herman and Clara could hear was the wind, but Abbey's ears caught another sound and at first she could not figure out what it was. It was high, higher than the wind. And it was sad and yet not quite like crying sad or unhappy sad. It was just like someone was lost and could not find his way in the storm.

She said to her father, "Daddy, there is someone out in the wind who is calling for help."

Herman huddled closer to Clara and to Abbey and said, "But I don't hear anything."

"But, Daddy, it really is there. I can hear it and someone is calling for help. We must go out and find him."

Now Herman had learned to trust his daughter. He thought of the danger that was waiting for them, but then he thought that maybe someone really was in danger and he knew Abbey could hear sounds that no one else could. So he said, "Very well, Abbey. We will go out in to the storm, but stay very close to me so you do not get blown away. Just keep nudging me the way we should go."

The two left Clara in the stable where she would be safe and they pushed their way into the snow and the wind. Abbey pushed her father straight ahead.

"I still hear the cry, Father." And Herman kept his strong body against the wind so little Abbey would not get blown away and the two of them moved farther and farther away from home. The snow was so blinding that neither one could see. But Abbey with her large ears could still hear the cry for help, so she nudged Herman closer and closer to the voice. Then suddenly there they were! In the storm they saw the blurred outline of a woman, sitting on a donkey that was just like Herman and a man trying to lead the donkey and calling into the wind, "Help! Help!"

Herman went up to the other donkey and pushed it toward the stable they had left. The other donkey, tired and frightened, was so very tired from walking in the storm and he was very happy to see Herman and more than glad to follow where he was led. The woman stayed sitting on the animal and the man grabbed Herman's tail so that he too could be led. Little Abbey stayed close to her father and the whole group at last came back to the stable where it was sheltered from the wind and the snow.

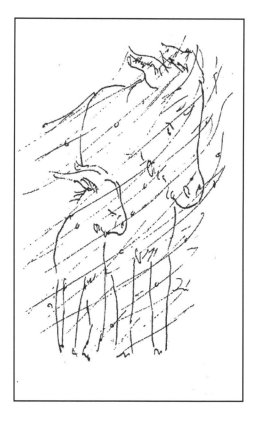

Abbey watched the man and the woman and she could not her eyes off of the pretty lady.

The pretty lady said to the man, "Joseph. It's time." And then she said to Abbey, "Wonderful little donkey, please make a bed of straw for us, because I am going to have a baby and I will need to have a place to put him down."

So Abbey took a big mouthful from the pile of straw that had not blown away, and she placed it in the manger. She used her nose to pat it down so that there would not be any rough spots or pieces of straw sticking up to hurt the little baby that was going to be born. While she was doing that, the pretty lady gave birth to a little boy baby.

And the pretty lady said to the man, "Look, Joseph. Here is Jesus." Joseph looked at the baby and smiled and then took the baby and placed him in the manger on the fresh straw that Abbey had made for them. When he had done that, Abbey walked over to the manger and breathed on the baby so that he would not catch cold in the windy stable.

Joseph stood along side of the manger on the side of Abbey and gently stroked her long ears. "If it had not been for you hearing my call for help, I do not know what would have happened to us. Thank you so much, Little Donkey. Never will the world forget what has happened this night when the baby was born and never will the world forget you and your courage. And never will the world forget the gift God gave you with such large ears so that you could hear a call for help in the storm."

Frankie the Frog

For Peggy O'Neill and the People of Suchitoto, El Salvador

Frankie the Frog had no idea how he got into the argument. He had been sitting very quietly on his lily pad, talking happily with Jellybean the Cow. They had been quite civil and polite in their conversation, discussing the clouds and the different shades of green of the trees. Then they had talked about the number of stars on a winter night and the funny way people walked on their two back legs. They also had talked about how strange it is that water does not get any wetter after a rainstorm and doesn't get any drier in the noontime sun. You know, all the important things that frogs and cows talk about when they have finished talking about the little things. They had come to that part in their conversation when a difference of opinion seems to take on greater importance than it really has.

Frankie the Frog had said that frogs had always gotten bad press because they could be turned into a prince when they got kissed by a big blond woman in a silly crown. He said it was very unfair that he might have to live his life walking on his two back legs and kissing big blonds with silly crowns. Jellybean the Cow had thought it rather

83

charming that a runty little frog could be chosen for such an adventure because no cow had ever been turned into a princess and would never be able to walk on her two back legs, although she couldn't image why she should want to.

"Runty little frog! You calling me a runty little frog?" Frankie shouted. "Runty little frog!" he repeated. He always thought that anything shouted once was worth shouting twice. This time, however, he outdid himself, and shouted a third time, "Runty little frog!"

Jellybean thought, "Oh, my. I seem to have gone too far on that one. Now he'll jump off his lily pad and won't come back for a week." Out loud she said, "Oh, I meant that as a compliment. It's not every frog that can be runty and still have an adventure."

Frankie stopped just before he could let out another cry. "Runty is good?" he asked.

"Oh, yes. It's very, very good," Jellybean answered. She was not too sure how she was going to get out of this one, but since she had started she knew she could not turn back now. "Haven't you ever heard of the adventure of Lester the Lizard? Or the adventure of Marvin the Mouse?"

"You're making this up," said Frankie because he had never heard of Lester the Lizard nor Marvin the Mouse and he was sure that he had heard all the stories Jellybean liked to tell. "If you are not making this up..." and he stared Jellybean right in the eyes, "If you aren't making this up, tell me about Marvin the Mouse and his adventure."

Jellybean lowered her head and then she shook it very, very slowly. "I wish you had not asked me about Marvin the Mouse," she finally said. "Marvin's adventure was a very strange one and I still have a hard time giving milk or going to sleep when I think of it."

"Ok, ok," said Frankie. "I don't have to give milk, but I would like to be able to sleep tonight so you don't have to tell me about Marvin. But I still want you to tell me about

84

a runty frog and why it's good to be runty."

Jellybean was in for it. She could have made up an interesting tale about the mouse and how, because he was small, he escaped the cat. And she could have told Frankie about how Lester was so small he confused the grasshopper. But what to do with a runty little frog?

She took a deep breath, rolled her eyes to heaven, and said a quick prayer to Saint Francis who always looked out for cows and frogs and other animals, "Well then. I shall tell you the story of Felipe the Frog who saved an entire village and could not have done it if he had not been small and runty."

"Felipe the Frog," exclaimed Frankie. "I like it already. Please go on and don't spare any of the frightening details."

Jellybean took another very deep breath, Saint Francis came through on time, and she then began the tale of Felipe the Frog.

"This all happened a long time ago and in a far away country," she said.

"How long ago and in what country?" interjected Frankie.

"I can't have you interrupting me all the time, Frankie. You may ask questions when I'm done, but I want to tell the story without you jumping in all the time. Is that clear?"

"Ok, it's clear," agreed Frankie, but he still wanted to know when and where this happened. Jellybean knew that he would not be able to listen properly until he knew when and where so she added, "This was at a time before you and I were born and it happened in a faraway place, so far away that it was called Suchitoto." The name was so magical to Frankie that he was speechless and could only settle more comfortably on his lily pad and listen.

Jellybean continued. "Well, in this far way time in the wonderful kingdom of Suchitoto, there lived a very small frog named Felipe. All of his brothers and sisters, all of his playmates, all of his school friends were much bigger than Felipe. They could jump from lily pad to lily pad with the greatest of ease, and they could jump out of the pond in a single leap. Felipe, however, frequently had to swim from one lily pad to another. And more often than not he would have to crawl out of the pond and rest for a bit from his exertions.

"All the other frogs wanted to laugh at Felipe, but they also really felt sorry for him and instead of laughing helped him when they could. For instance, Glenda, the biggest frog in the pond, often stayed close to Felipe and let him jump off a lily pad onto her back and then on to the next lily pad. She pretended that she was tired and simply wanted to rest where she was, but really she just wanted Felipe to keep up with the other frogs and not get left behind.

"Well one day, in this far away kingdom of Suchitoto, the clouds moved in over the Guazapa mountains in a very unusual way. First there were little puffy clouds, then there were bigger heavy clouds, and finally there were huge, dark, and menacing clouds. And there was no thunder. Everyone knows that clouds bring storms and that there is always thunder with the storm. But this time there were frightening clouds and not a sound from the heavens. In fact, it was deathly quiet. Even as the clouds got bigger and darker, the wind became quieter and quieter. All the animals began to ask each other what this meant. The robins asked the sparrows, the sparrows asked the raccoons, the raccoons asked the monkeys, the monkeys asked the horses, and the horses asked the oxen. And not one of them knew why the sky was so dark and the land itself so quiet.

"Felipe was just as scared as everyone else. He looked at the sky and he looked around him. He saw that Glenda, even though she was big, was also frightened. Then it began to rain in a very unusual way. First there was a mist of water that was unlike any other mist they had ever seen; a heavy mist which drenched everything immediately. And then the mist turned into rain, but it was a different kind of rain. The drops were sharp, almost as sharp as needles and as large as marsh reeds. The sky got darker and the rain turned into swirling water instead of just coming down like rain is supposed to. Everyone knew that something awful was about to happen. But they had no name for it and they had never seen anything like it before. Felipe, just as scared as the others, jumped off his lily pad, crawled out of the pond, and lied close to the ground to listen. Because he was so small, he could hear what the rain was saying to the ground and what the ground was saying to the rain. They told each other that the mountains would not be able to hold all the waters and that the ground could not drink up all the waters. They told each other that a terrible flood was about to come into the Kingdom of Suchitoto. They must all flee and find safety.

"Felipe quickly told Glenda and Glenda told the other animals, 'A terrible flood is coming. Everyone find a safe place and wait for it to pass. Quickly! Quickly!'

"Then Glenda and the other frogs dove deep into the pond; the robins and sparrows flew into the caves; the monkeys and raccoons climbed tall trees and sheltered themselves under the big branches. Everyone, in fact, ran for the safest place to be found. Everyone, that is, except Felipe. He thought to himself, 'The huge animals that walk on their two back legs need to find safety too. I must warn them.'

"But how? How could a runty little frog warn the huge animals that walk on their two back legs that they were in danger? 'I do not know how I will do it, but I must try,' Felipe said to himself. He watched as the rain began to form little streams and flowed down the hillside. Then an idea came to him. 'Since I am so small, a leaf can carry me down the hillside to where the huge animals live and I can tell them they must flee before it's too late.'

"So Felipe watched for a leaf to come by that was just the right size. He jumped on it as though it was one of his lily pads, and the waters began to carry him down, down, down the hillside. Sometimes he almost fell off and at other times the leaf almost got stuck on a branch or on a bigger leaf. But Felipe hung on and he pushed the bigger leaves to the side and kept on riding down the hillside to give his warning of danger.

"Pretty soon, although it could never be soon enough for Felipe, he saw a light farther down the hill. 'The huge animals who walk on their back legs live there,' he said to himself. 'I will get off of my leaf and tell them.' Which is exactly what he did. He waited for the leaf to pause ever so slightly as it flowed past a fallen branch and he jumped off. He hopped as quickly as he could to where he had seen the light. But the door was closed and all the windows sealed against the rain. At first, he almost cried with frustration and disappointment. But he knew he couldn't stop now. He jumped up on the step and he saw that there was just a little sliver of light coming under the door. 'Maybe,' he thought, 'maybe I can push through.' So he got down as small as he could. But he was too big to slide through the opening. So he pushed himself even harder against the floor and then with all his might used his back legs to force himself under the door. He tried to make himself as small as he could and then perhaps even smaller. He just had to warn whoever was behind the door. Then, with all the strength he could gather, he pushed one last time. The opening was so small that Felipe scraped his back and he scraped his stomach, but he just made it through the tiny gap.

"Tired and frightened and hurt, he looked in the room and saw an old man sitting by the fire. He was just sitting quietly on a little stool, sharpening his machete, barely moving and probably not even listening to the wind and the rain that was falling outside the house. Felipe croaked at him as loudly as he could. And still the man did not notice. Felipe took another big breath and croaked again, even louder than he thought was possible. And still the man seemed not to hear. Felipe jumped over and sat on the old man's shoe and croaked a third time. The old man looked at his shoe, since his face was aiming in that direction anyway, and he saw that a frog was sitting there looking up at him and croaking a very loud message.

"Now the man was so old that he had lived through other times, times that were both much better and much worse. And he knew that frogs do not come into one's house and sit on one's shoe and croak. So he knew something must be wrong. He tried to remember something that was just on the edge of his memory and would not come easily. He looked at Felipe, although he did not know that Felipe was his name, and he thought some more.

"And then it came to him. A Flood! Yes, that was it. There was going to be a flood. The last time a frog had come into his house and croaked was when the mountain poured down all the rain it had gathered over a long winter and washed away all the houses and ruined all the fields. He grabbed his straw hat and he ran out the door. He ran down the hillside until he came to the houses below. "A flood is coming," he shouted. "A flood is coming. A little runty frog has warned me and I am warning you: a flood is coming." Then all the people grabbed their blankets and their children and their chickens and they ran for higher ground where the flood would not reach them. And there they were safe and they stayed there until the flood passed and they could return to their homes. Not one of them was hurt because Felipe has been so brave."

Frankie waited a moment and he just could not hold the question back. "And how did Felipe get back to his own pond and his own lily pads?"

89

Jellybean smiled and said, "Ah, that is the work of another story which I shall tell you some other time."

"But..." Frankie blurted out.

"Some other time," Jellybean said, emphasizing each syllable, making it sound like a threat. "All you need to know is that if Felipe had not been a frog and had not been a runty little frog, the whole village of Suchitoto would have been destroyed and there would be no story to tell in the first place."

"All right," said Frankie. "I'll wait for the next story but I really want to know how Felipe got home."

"I'll remember that," said Jellybean. The two friends looked at each for a moment in silence, and then Jellybean said, "Goodnight, Frankie."

And Frankie said, "Goodnight, Jellybean." He then jumped off of his lily pad into the pond. Jellybean smiled to herself and said "Goodnight" again to the empty air and then walked slowly back to her barn.

The Bishop Thumps

Rumors, the very life line of reality in the diocese, were rife. The old bishop had merely to cough and the mills of hope and desire churned into life and ground each morsel of news into the bread of truth. The next bishop would be a man of canon law and would return order and discipline into the ranks of the Church. No, he would be a man who would carry on the usually progressive plans of the old man, although those plans were often marred by indecision and even, sometimes, indifference. The new bishop would come from the diocese itself and would be someone that the priests could respect. No, he would come from outside and give no one an inside track. He would be a caretaker until someone more suitable could be found. No, he would be young enough to accomplish something and not just wait around for death. It was all wonderfully speculative and clerical.

Rumor has a way of proving itself true, and each faint innuendo was credited with mystic insight. The old bishop sent forth his ghost on the wave of a hiccup, was buried with proper solemnity and at the clergy dinner following the funeral, set in motion the process of rewarding the pundits of clerical astuteness with the laurel of victory. The Delphic Oracle breathed forth and an unknown outsider was chosen.

He was young — relatively — and considered a progressive in a very regressive large archdiocese. He was one of those who had been specially picked out by the apostolic delegate as one of the bright, new lights in the American church. The possibilities were endless for an admixture of past performance and future achievement. True, nothing notable had been reported on either side of the ledger so that those prone to clericalism in all its wonder could only continue their speculations. All, they felt, would be proved by the installation, the keynote speech, and the dinner afterwards.

But clarity can be fickle and only those who lie or who have returned from the dead can claim prescience. The new bishop appeared, as if by alchemy, at the Chancery Office one day— a good ten days before he was expected. Now the Chancery itself is an imposing structure. Modern, marble, efficient, desks where desks should be, corridors and doors exactly as they were drawn on the designer's board. The receptionist's well was central to the whole operation. She could see who came in before the visitor knew that he was found out, and then he had to walk several yards into the room before he could hope to make his request known. And even then he was not assured of success in his given mission. The secretary's fingers were hidden from view so that any number of buttons or combination of buttons could be pushed and the visitor would never know if he were being received or ejected or, possibly, arrested.

But the new bishop need not have feared. His picture had become public property for the past several weeks and he was instantly recognized. What he did not know, and could not know, was the frantic fingering of the switchboard console, for the secretary was playing her instrument like a concert pianist, playing in the key of Panic. By the time the bishop got to the desk, doors were flying open, corridors were full, the Muzak sound system was hushed, and the Chancellor was standing alongside of him, bending over to kiss his ring.

The only feature of the bishop's face that changed from its granite warmth was a slightly arched eyebrow. He took the extraordinary reception as his ordinary due, gave his ring, which was not incidentally on a well manicured hand, to be kissed, and only then said, smilingly, "Ah, I see I have been recognized. Can't sneak around here, he-he." It would be a matter of moments when the bishop's 'he-he' would be interpreted for what it was, not the gentle chuckle of a happy man but the first warning growl of a dangerous animal. At this first moment, however, it was benignly received.

The Chancellor had recovered by this time and rose to the occasion. "Welcome, Bishop. We were not expecting you so soon but are indeed glad that you are here."

"Please show me to my office, Father."

"Of course, Bishop. Right this way." And then the journey began. The two clerics walked silently past the secretary, past the priests who had clustered around, waiting to be introduced, past the other office workers, past the typists, the janitors, the maintenance men, past the whole population of the Chancery world from 8:30 a.m. to 4:30 p.m. They passed through the huge arch that would, if it could, embrace the whole of the complex, down the long marble corridor of spotless existence, through an enormous walnut door, into a sumptuous reception room, and finally into a cavernous room which would be only one spot on earth: the bishop's office.

The bishop looked around him. He took in the pictures on the walls, the heavy oriental carpet, the soft leather chairs and couches, the bookcases, empty of the former bishop's library, and the desk. Here more than one diocesan wag had wondered how many football games could be played upon that desktop at the same time. Three was the generally accepted number. Without another word, the bishop walked around the desk, pushed the leather swivel chair a few times to make sure there was no noise, and then sat down as though it were an action he had performed at that same desk at that same spot since time immemorial.

The two men had said nothing to each other on the trek to the heart of the Chancery. That silence was now broken by the bishop. "Well, Father. Here we are. There are two requests I have for the present. The first is that I expect the resignations of all those who work at the Chancery before this week is out, and second, I want a list of all those churches in my diocese which are under construction—any stage of construction or renovation. That list is to be on my desk by morning.

"I believe that is sufficient for today." He rose from the desk, rather like Venus doing her dawn bit, and looked around him. "Is there another exit here, Father?" he asked.

"Yes, Bishop. There is a door over there which you can use when you want to come or go without being seen."

"Fine. I'll just go that way now. And, Father, there is no need to tell anyone I have left."

It was a matter of seconds and the Chancellor found himself alone in the office. For a moment he just stood there, looking at the closed door. He blinked a few times which helped him collect himself. He then turned and left the room. He returned to his own office, sat at his desk, and stared at nothing for a few moments. He then called in his secretary and dictated a short note.

"'To all personnel. The Bishop has requested that all personnel hand in their resignations from any position they now hold in the Chancery, effective Monday, March 13th. They may be given to Miss Armster, who will give them to me.' And just sign my name."

"Does this mean everyone?" Miss Armster wondered

aloud.

"Everyone. I believe our bishop wants to start with a new broom and that he just came today to get the sweeping under way. I have a feeling Madeleine, that things are going to be different around here from now on. He's gone for now (and then he felt a tinge of guilt that he had made his first betrayal) but he'll be back tomorrow."

As Miss Armster turned to leave, the chancellor remembered his other directive. "Oh, and, Madeleine. Please call the office for buildings and have them get a list of all the churches that are under construction or are being renovated. The bishop wants the list when he comes in tomorrow. You had better have them also send in the names of churches that have made requests for renovations too. And please don't look at me like that. I haven't got the vaguest idea what's going on either." The Chancellor found no comfort in admitting his bewilderment. Nor did he doubt that Miss Armster would have the list neatly typed before she left the Chancery for the evening.

The air in the chancery that next morning fairly bristled with anticipation. The talking was hushed and limited to A-Need-To-Know basis and the laughter was muted into extinction. At precisely 8:30 the bishop walked into the Chancellor's office. His 'good morning' was curt, peremptory, and invited no return greeting. "You have the list, Father?" Even the way the question was asked left no possibility of a negative answer.

"Yes, Bishop. It's right here."

There followed a moment of intense scrutiny as the bishop looked at the list. "You don't have the projected dates for completion here, I see. Which of these churches is closest to being finished?"

The Chancellor looked at the list and said, "St. Matthew's is planning on opening its doors for the first time at Easter, Bishop. Father Henry Simpson was just waiting for the announcement of the new bishop before he

95

set the date for the dedication. But the church is almost finished now."

"Suppose we pay a visit to, what was his name, Simpson?"

"Now, Bishop?"

The look on the bishop's face shouted, Now! He said nothing however. He simply turned and walked toward his own office.

The Chancellor quickly placed his brief call to St. Matthew's, grabbed his own coat and ran after the bishop. By the time he got to the bishop's office, the bishop already had his coat on and was waiting. "You drive, Father."

The two men walked through the private exit, got into the car and were half way to St. Matthew's before a word was spoken. "I used be at St. Matthew's, Bishop. In fact, it was my first assignment. It will be good to see what's happened there," said the Chancellor.

Any hope of conversation died when the bishop responded, "I know, Father. I've read your dossier."

Eventually the car pulled up in front of the new church. There were construction trucks, workers, scaffolds, sand and mud all clustered around the new walls of brick and glass. But clearly, the church was in its final stage of birth and a concerted effort would quickly bring the building into full flower. Without looking at anything in particular but noticing everything, the bishop walked through the main door and walked to the middle of the church before he stopped.

He looked around rather briefly and then he began to stare at the floor. At this stage of construction, the floor was still simply rough poured concrete and it laid there, rather ugly and gray. He just shook his head slightly as though denying to himself the reality his eyes beheld. By this time, Father Simpson had joined them. The Chancellor made the introductions and then stood back and waited. There was a long pause during which the sound of pounding could be heard. "And what kind of floor are you going to have, Father?" the bishop asked.

Father Simpson was galvanized into action. The whole church was built around a very simple concept: the colors and materials of the walls and furnishings would all be brought together with the neutral color carpet. The rather severe lines of the building would retain their functionality at the same time lose none of their elegance. The pastor was just beginning to explain this when he was interrupted. "No, Father. Terrazzo."

Father Simpson was stunned. "Terrazzo, Bishop? The architect told us that any hard surface would be all wrong. He especially said that terrazzo would be very expensive and would be completely out of place for here. We have a lot of older people in the parish and in winter they would slip and could easily hurt themselves on any hard surface like terrazzo. Besides, we'd have to redo the entire floor. We've planned for carpet and," here he hoped he had the winning argument on his side, "carpet was approved by the diocesan consultants." He was stopped from further explanation by the bishop's impatience.

"No, Father. Terrazzo! I will speak with the consultants about this immediately. You needn't worry. You don't seem to understand. When I enter my churches, the people want to know that their bishop is in the building. When I bang my crosier on the floor, people want to hear it. They want to know that their representative before God is present. The crosier does not bang on a carpet, only on terrazzo." He looked once more at the floor. "No, Father. Terrazzo. I would hate to have another priest as pastor here when you have done so much for getting the church built."

Both listeners thought that, among the many things this new bishop hated, removing a pastor on the spot was not on the list.

Without another word, the bishop turned and walked out of the building. The two remaining priests looked at each other for a moment, hovering between tears of rage or of hysterical laughter. "My God," the Chancellor said. "This one's a banger!" It was all that was needed for the laughter to win out.

By noon of the same day, word was out all over the diocese: the bishop thumps.

Bishop at Bay

Father Welton was just coming in from the garage with his golf clubs hung over his arm when his secretary met him at the door, "The Bishop is on the phone." The man always wanted something, like why the numbers for the Peter's Pence collection were down, why the entire parish had not subscribed to the diocesan paper, why he hadn't been at the last presbytery meeting; all very critical and burning issues that Father Welton felt quite free to ignore. Until, of course, there was a phone call and then a list of immediate reasons would be forthcoming, on why it was simply impossible: a funeral, a bout of lumbago, the sky had fallen and Chicken Little was right. It was all part of the game at which the Bishop and he were masters. Authority and submission, action and reaction, guilt induced and rejected.

"Please tell him that I will be right there, Frances," said Father Welton. But what he thought was, "Dammit, there goes my free day."

Father Welton deserved his free day. It was Easter Week and he had just been through the usual frenzy called the High Liturgy of Holy Week. There had been the Palm

Sunday with its waving of palms all during the Gospel and the ensuing parade, called liturgically a procession, in which the teenagers never came back for the rest of Mass and the faithful faithfully read their lines from the crumpled missalettes. Palm Sunday set the tone for the rest of the celebrations of Holy Thursday, Good Friday, and the blessing of the Pascal Candle and lighting the Easter fire at the Vigil. There also had been the confessions and the supervising of the Easter decorations which always managed to make the church smell like a funeral parlor. This year on Holy Thursday he added an ecumenical service with several of the Protestant denominations in a rather lovely affair held in the large Methodist church two blocks away. But when the effects of the week were added together, Father Welton would have gladly settled for a Mass said in some cloistered convent on the edge of oblivion.

He deserved his day off this week and to have it interrupted by the Bishop with some nicety of Canon Law was not his idea of clerical fun and frolic during the Holy Season. He closed the door to his office as he slung his golf bags off his shoulder.

"Hello, Bishop. How nice of you to call." That should set the tone, he thought, and keep it light.

"Yes, yes, well," the Bishop responded. It struck Father Welton that there was an edge to his gravely voice, which probably meant that he had received the Good Friday Holy Land collection and wasn't pleased. "Happy Easter, Father, and we have something very serious to talk about."

The Bishop did not know the meaning of serious. Everything had to be 'very serious' or it did not exist. Father Welton could see him shaking his head on the two words so that his jowls, very ample jowls at that, would quiver and give the Bishop's critics the justifiable opportunity to compare him to a Shar-Pei puppy.

The Bishop had been trained by the best, The Boss. His rise in the chancery office had been steady if not particularly spectacular and The Boss had kept his eye on him. He was liked for his fundraising abilities and his talent for moving in higher social circles without upstaging The Boss. When he came to the small Southern diocese, it was with the understanding that it would be a temporary assignment and that Rome would certainly want to give him The Boss's job when it became available. The Boss had died. Another chancery man got the job and the Bishop was still in the South waiting, although he would have used the term "languishing". But he wanted to be sure that there would be no mar on his ability to rule, raise funds, and keep his priests in line. And there certainly would not be any of that ecumenical nonsense which watered down the True Church. Jesus was definitely a Catholic and no one should be in doubt.

Father Welton considered the Bishop's Happy Easter the spoonful of sugar which was supposed to make the medicine go down. "I have a report here on my desk with some very serious allegations about you." And then silence. Father Welton, figuring that he would find out soon enough what those allegations were, managed a non-committal.

"Oh?" He said, just to keep the phone from sounding too dead.

"Yes, very serious indeed," came from the other end. Father Welton felt as though he were being told to take off his shoes because he was on holy ground.

"Who are the allegations from, Bishop?" he finally asked more for something to say rather than from real interest. It was well known that the CIA and the KGB were bungling amateurs when it came to the Bishop and his stable of informants. It was equally well known that he protected his sources with a fidelity and zeal that would make a St. Stephen jealous.

"That doesn't matter, Father. The report says, and if this is true it is very serious, that you said Mass in a Protestant church with a Protestant minister without my permission." Even the laypeople in the diocese knew that the Bishop's ecumenical fervor was matched only by the Ayatollah Khomeini's. So there he was, the Bishop who blessed bombs for the troops, being self-righteous and a stalwart of the faith because a priest of the diocese had prayed with other Christians.

"We did have an ecumenical service, Bishop, on Holy Thursday, but I think you will find it was a very reverent and simple service and Catholic doctrine was not compromised in any way. And it was according to the norms of documents on the liturgy which came out of Rome."

"You should have gotten my permission before you did that. That's in the documents that came out of Rome too."

Oh, well. There it was again, thought Father Welton. It wasn't the theology, or the service, or even the ecumenism; it was the lack of permission. I never thought to get permission. Permissions had never been Father Welton's strong suit. He figured that if you had to ask you probably didn't know what you were asking for and you were expecting someone else to take the responsibility. He had been through the same seminary courses, had the same theology and Canon Law degrees as the Bishop did and never felt that theology was a matter of permissions. This issue had come up several times in his history and he always felt he was on the side of the angels if not on that of the Bishop.

"Well, we just can't have this, can't have it at all," said the Bishop, and he did nothing to hide the nasty bite in his words.

This time, something happened to Father Welton. He was tired and he was frustrated. His eyes became hard and his manner cool as he knew with a terrible clarity what he would do. He said in a voice that was slow and deliberate, tinged with just a hint of patronization, "I am very sorry, Bishop. I certainly would not want to give a bad impression of the Church. It is well known how hard you have worked for the Catholics in this area and I would not want to damage all of the good work you have done. And I agree: it would be very bad if it came out in the papers that permission had not been obtained before the service. I know how careful we have to be of the press and how eager they are to discredit anything Catholic."

Here, Father Welton took a deep breath. He could still retreat into the banalities the Bishop loved. But this time he could feel the adrenalin rising and he went with the flow. "It would almost be as bad as if the press found out that there were financial irregularities in the diocese."

It was a shot, and not a very long one either. It was rumored in the diocesan underground that some of the Bishop's financial dealings were not what would look good when scrutinized by the IRS, or even the diocesan Board of Advisors. Recently the pastor of the neighboring parish had been removed because of 'fiscal irresponsibility' because he had diverted parish funds into a soup kitchen. The Bishop had been livid and then covered the money with funds from the diocese, never telling anyone where the funds had come from. His ire was focused on the money going to a soup kitchen when it could have been used to build something, anything. He covered the expenses because he did not want anyone to think that the Church could not pay its bills. What happens in an autocracy does not always look good in the light of a democratic press.

Neither man spoke, both holding their phones to their ears to listen to the other's silence. Father Welton sat quietly at his desk and waited. No matter what it cost him, he would not be the first to break that silence. Presently the Bishop cleared his throat with a sound somewhere between a growl and grunt and said, "I expect a full report of the incident on my desk by tomorrow morning... and next time, get my permission," and slammed the phone down.

The gamble had worked. Father Welton sat there and gently put the phone back in its cradle. His face was blank until a slight smile warmed it. Well, that's that, he thought. I suppose that I will have to do some sort of a report for him to show his toadies in the chancery office. As he placed his golf clubs back in the closet, a very pleasant idea struck him. Next time perhaps, he thought, we can talk about the priests who have mistresses.

Monsignor as One

Monsignor Hanson watched from his study window as his curate jogged up the path. It was the only blight on the scene of swept sidewalks, manicured lawns, and bright flowers all disciplined into submission outlining the building. But Monsignor was not pleased, not pleased at all. And the orderly world of Saint Andrew's was being destroyed — yes, destroyed — by this upstart. "I warned him," he said to himself but his thought was as loud on his face as if he had shouted out the window. "I warned him."

Father Wycek was hot and sweaty from jogging. He had been exercising along the canal again, a place he had been told to avoid and for his own good too. There were so many things he had been told for his own good, like jogging itself. Monsignor had even offered to give Father a membership in the health club that he belonged to, and the offer had been refused. It was preposterous.

Monsignor thought to himself, "I'll have to tell This One about him too." He always thought of the bishop as One. The First One had been the bishop who ordained him; That One was the previous bishop; This One now held the office. And it was the firm expectation of Monsignor's constant hope and faith in the wisdom of the Church that he too would become One. And especially now that there were rumblings that This One was going to ask for an auxiliary.

And why not? Monsignor had served the Church well over the years. He had built two churches and remodeled another, which were all now considered "plums" in the diocese. They were imposing structures, like Saint Andrew's for instance. It had taken several fund drives and much reluctance on the part of the parishioners, but the work was done. He could look out his window and see the fruits of his labors and realize that no one else in the diocese could boast such productivity. Well, he would be ready when the time came to show This One that he could do the same thing for the whole diocese. It would not be easy of course, but he would be willing to spend his last days directing the affairs of souls from his episcopal throne.

No, it wouldn't be easy. But Monsignor felt equal to the task. As he looked at Father Wycek now, just rounding the corner of the building toward the back door, he could not suppress a quiet smile at what he would do with such a curate if he had the opportunity to reassign him. Their relationship had never realized the level that Monsignor had expected. The club membership was only one thing and there had been so many others. Nothing open or surly, mind you, just constant and vexing. Like the use of names, for example. At their first meeting, Father Wycek had called Monsignor Tom. Tom! No one had dared use that name with him since he left for the seminary. Monsignor had looked him steadily in the eye and said, not coldly or unkindly, "It is better for the image of the Church if you simply called me Monsignor."

Father Wycek looked at him, his head just slightly cocked, a cross between wonder and amusement on his face and said, "As you wish."

Since that time, he had called him absolutely nothing. His answers to questions became positively biblical:

106

yea-yea, or nay-nay, and never a title along with it. That sort of thing could be infuriating without being disrespectful. This Wycek had much to learn and he seemed to be a slow learner.

There had been a moment of slight compunction, just after he had written to This One about having written, although he had not mailed the letter yet. It had happened before and now it was happening again, but if the Church were to retain its hold on the people, This One just had to be informed that the young men coming out of the seminary were not what they used to be. It was for their own good too, although they never saw it that way. The letter had been simple and straightforward, no embellishments, no hysteria, no name-calling, just the facts: Father Wycek was fundamentally unfit to be curate at a parish like Saint Andrew's. The people expected more and Monsignor had taught them they had a right to their expectations. Father Wycek just could not see that it was for his own good that he should keep his distance. Why, he even permitted the altar boys to call him by his first name! What possible effect could come but that the Church would suffer from such familiarity, which Monsignor knew bred contempt. And that he would not allow. So the letter requesting an appointment would have to be sent, ,and four times before there had been results with curates. So there was every reason to expect that this letter also would achieve its intended goal.

It was always a tiresome time before a new curate was appointed. Monsignor had all of the Masses, except for the Supply he would get from the religious orders in the city. He always took the 7:00 a.m. Mass and there was never a homily at that service because, as Monsignor pointed out, the working people had to get to their jobs. But all the phone calls, all the hospital visits, all the meetings had to be conducted by Monsignor who should have been preparing himself for more weighty tasks. He considered it a sign of his administrative abilities that he could take care of all the work of the parish between 10:30 and 11:45 on weekday mornings, except for the incoming phone calls of course, but the secretary could and did take messages. Administration was the key. And it was that administrative genius, he knew, which could be used for the whole diocese and not just one part of it.

He was so lost in his thoughts that he did not hear the door open behind him. "Ah, there you are." Again, no title. Always you. Or in overheard conversations, him. "Do you want me to take the afternoon or evening shift for confessions?"

Monsignor did not like to have his authority undermined like that. It was only fitting that he announce at lunch the schedule for the weekend and not have this haphazard exchange of information as though equals were conversing about equal tasks. It, like Father Wycek himself, would just not do.

"There are some things I have to attend to, so you had better take them both, Father." He tried not to let the italics sound in his voice on the title, but he knew it was there. Maybe it was just as well.

The two men looked at each other, both expectant of something more from the other. But there was no more. Both knew that the "things to attend to" had not yet received even intentional existence but Monsignor was at the advantage; he would think of something. Since there seemed to be no more words to dangle at each other, Father Wycek turned and walked out of the room.

Monsignor felt that he had scored his point, but he wasn't sure. He had a vague feeling that Father Wycek had won that round and somehow, the conversation had not gone the way he wanted it to. If he had had any doubts about sending the letter to That One, they had vanished in the past few minutes. It was for the good of the Church that Father Wycek learn his place and better sooner than later, better at some other parish than at Saint Andrew's. "I will not have my record marred by a smart alack upstart. When the review board looks at my file, there can be nothing in it which will give them second thoughts about my ability to rule and get the respect the Church demands." Monsignor felt fully confident and sure of himself, and more than just a little pleased. "It is, after all, for the good of the Church."

The "things to attend to" turned out to be driving to the downtown post office. The letter would reach the Chancery Office on Monday morning, a good time before the hectic schedule began for the week. He fed the slot one immaculate heavily-bonded envelope with the six lines of type on the face: name, title, diocese, chancery office, street address, and city with the state and zip code all on their proper lines. On the left side, in clear, capital letters was the single word PERSONAL. It was an impressive looking envelope, just the kind that he also would like to receive some day. To Monsignor's watchful eye, the slot itself seemed grateful to be trusted with such a mission as there was just a hint of a whisper as the letter slid to rest with the great machinery of government which promised total confidentiality. "Not unlike the confessions Father Wycek is hearing right now," he thought but then let the thought slip away like the envelope. It did not pay to set the hand to the plow and look backwards.

Saturday night was uneventful. The meal was an impeccably cooked rare roast beef, impeccably served and ritually mumbled over in gratitude. The Lord was reminded that Monsignor and his guests (Father Wycek was the only other person present) were not unmindful of the poor who had nothing to eat and that He is the Giver of all good gifts. Once Father Wycek had been asked to lead the prayer and Monsignor could only listen in shocked disbelief. The image of migrant workers, strikers, tramps, and drunks had been brought into the dining room to taint the reverent atmosphere. After that, Monsignor retained his privilege as pastor to conduct the invocations.

Conversation had never been easy between the two and both were allowed to dine within their respective invisible bubbles. During the salad, Monsignor remained poised to answer any questions about difficult penitents that might come up, although none ever did. There had been a question once, early in Father Wycek's stay, about a teenage pregnancy. He had taken the opportunity to lecture Father on the dangers of sexuality, although he never actually used the word, and somehow the teenager had gotten lost in the lecture. But the Church's clear stand had been upheld and loyalty to the Holy Father had been vigorously reaffirmed in the process. Conversation after that had dwindled until the present state of quiet which, Monsignor interpreted, once more displayed Father Wycek's ineptitude at the social graces so necessary for a leader of the people at Saint Andrew's.

The Lord was again reminded that eternal rest to all the faithfully departed was expected and the meal was over. Nothing was said about the evening confessions as the two men rose; the necessity of scanning the morning's conversation did not arise.

Sunday was a normal day of Masses and rest. After the seven o'clock service, Monsignor retired to his office to await the ushers who brought in the collection with a hush of reverence and obeisance that sustained the mystery of the liturgy itself. And then he watched as they opened the envelopes, counted and bundled the money in neat little stacks and listened indulgently as they commented on the financial state of the parish. "That same one is back who rolls up the dollar bill like a toothpick." "Fifties are down." "Not as good as last week."

Comforting and secure statements bounced like angel wings around the office, punctuated by the steady metallic sound of the coin machine going its appointed rounds. Figures were entered neatly into columns of the ledger as though there were an implicit race among the different Masses each Sunday and between the same Masses on different Sundays. It was all there in the ledger and made tabulation simple when the yearly contributors' sheet was published. The beauty of administration was everywhere present and accounted for.

On Monday, Monsignor came down to this office at 10:30 as usual. The secretary had already opened the mail so he had to merely slide the letters, or bills, or requests neatly out of their envelopes. Some he dispatched to the secretary for checks, others to the secretary for baptismal certificates, still others went back to the secretary for filing. It was the work of a moment to have everything placed in its proper place in the universe of the well-run parish. And then he waited. He knew that the Chancery got its mail at roughly the same time as he got his. So right now his letter should be receiving the attention he expected it to deserve. He never knew if This One's secretary opened and read the mail or if she merely opened it. But she was discreet. At least she had never given Monsignor a lagniappe that had come across her desk, and if he did not get an occasional inside peek at the written inner-workings of the diocese, who would? Therefore he had no reason to suspect her discretion.

The phone rang. Monsignor waited for the secretary to inform him of an incoming call on Line One. The intercom button lit up, but the buzzing sound went off in Father Wycek's office. "I hope he doesn't talk too long," Monsignor thought. Perhaps he should inform the secretary that only calls to him and those from the Chancery Office should be put through. No, that would be to tip his hand and he was not willing to do that yet.

The light went off on Line One, and Monsignor watched the indolent instrument on his desk. He toyed with his appointment book and flipped the blank pages back and forth. The only marking on his calendar for the week was on Wednesday, 2:30 golf with Mr. Dowling, the most generous giver at Saint Andrew's. Monsignor liked to let him win. Give him the upper hand in golf and he would take the upper hand in Church matters; it was a simple and uncostly tradeoff.

But still the phone remained in semi-retirement well into the afternoon. There had been four calls for Father Wycek and one for him, requesting permission to have a wedding in another parish. As soon as Monsignor was confident that no further business would be conducted from the Chancery that day, he went to his room to think of the possible options that faced him. Perhaps the letter had not gotten there today; perhaps This One wanted more time to consider its contents; perhaps the list of possible curates was being poured over and the choicest ones were being set aside for election. Perhaps... But there were no more perhapses; Monsignor could think of no other alternatives.

Tuesday was a day of intensified frustration. Nothing important came to the rectory, nothing that could not be handled perfunctorily with an immediate decision of rapier-like swiftness. Maybe the letter had been lost! He had not thought of that yesterday and even now he could not believe that the government, which he had elected into office, would play so foul a trick on him with such a crucial message. No, no. The trouble was at the Chancery; that was clear. But what kind of trouble?

Wednesday would have to be the day of action. If he did not get a call from the Chancery Office, he would have to do the calling. The mere thought of that irked him because it put him in the suppliant's role, and he was the one who was doing the diocese a favor by exposing Father Wycek's unsuitableness. After all, what if Father Wycek were to be considered for a pastorate within the next few years? That would not be for the good of the Church at all. Even though the number of active priests was dwindling, it was better for the Church to have fewer priests than to allow men of Father Wycek's stripe to exert leadership over a confused Church.

Monsignor could tolerate the Chancery's silence no longer. Since it was for the good of the Church that he had taken his stand, he should be willing to humble himself, at least a little, and make the call himself. Just as his resolve was firmed to the point of irrevocability, Line One blinked and a ring was heard in the secretary's office. He had a premonition that this was it, and he was not disappointed this time.

After a short pause, his buzzer rang and he heard, "Monsignor, you have a call on Line One, please. It's Mrs. Langley from the Chancery."

He tried not to sound either too surprised or too expectant as he said, "Thank you. I'll take it." Mrs. Langley, This One's personal secretary at last!

The conversation was short: Would it be convenient for Monsignor to come to the Chancery Office this afternoon at three? A few things I would have to reschedule (this looking at the lonely golf date) but, yes, it could be arranged. Thank you. Good-bye, Monsignor.

The early afternoon was eternal and Monsignor was listless. Finally, he showered and put on an iron-starched shirt with blindingly white French cuffs under his clerical collar. The bold touch of purple under the stiff white of the collar proclaimed in an understated manner his dignity within the Household of the Pope. He was, all in all, quite prepared to see the purple expanded and a tasteful pectoral cross on a level with his armpits, and in his imagination it was already there. A quick brush on the shoulders and on the trousers of his new black wool suit, a steady gaze at himself in the full length mirror behind his closet door, and he was ready.

He went to the phone, dialed Mr. Dowling's private number, and said in a slightly breathless voice, "Sorry, Ted, but something came up. His Excellency wants to see me on something pretty important right away. I don't know what it is, but he sounded pretty excited." The double lie hung in the air for both to consider, pretending it was the weight of This One's urgent business that always threatened their engagements and kept even their friendship on a tentative footing.

"Maybe next Wednesday, huh, Monsignor?"

"Maybe next Wednesday," came the reply, which managed to hint at business so encompassing that every Wednesday for the next year would be at Episcopal disposal.

At precisely 2:57, Monsignor pulled into the Chancery parking lot. At 2:58 he entered the elevator. At 2:59 he announced his presence to Mrs. Langley. Punctuality had always been his pride. No matter what else was happening in the world, punctuality was essential for effective and efficient administration. "Please take a seat, Monsignor. The bishop is busy right now and will see you in a moment." She continued her typing, answered a few phone calls, took messages and gave no hint of her knowledge or ignorance of Monsignor's mission.

The moment became minutes, seventeen and a half of them. Monsignor remained outwardly composed through this period although he felt the tension of the past four days tightening within him; ever since, in fact, he had entrusted his letter to the post office. He pretended a calmness he in no way felt as he picked through the magazines in the waiting room. Finally Mrs. Langley's intercom rang. She picked up the phone and said in her rather flat, efficient voice. "Yes, Bishop. Monsignor Hanson is here." There was a brief pause, then "Yes, Bishop." As she placed the receiver gently in its cradle, she said, "The Bishop will see you now."

Monsignor had the air of one who would have gladly replied, "About time, too!" But all he did say was, "Yes. Well, thank you." He walked with a faintly military stride to the heavy dark door, rapped twice in a firm manner (once would have sounded hesitant and might be interpreted as timidity; thrice would have sounded too anxious; twice managed to announce his presence and at the same time remain neutral to misinterpretation). The door was partially open when the words "Come in" were heard.

Monsignor was already half way in the room before he realized that he was joining a meeting already in progress. Father Mark Quigley, the newly elected personnel director, was already sitting in the chair along side of This One's desk. Monsignor was surprised that Father Quigley should be there; why the personnel director? His election by the priests of the diocese was something Monsignor did not approve of: it smacked of democracy in the Church and, as he often reminded his parishioners, the Church is not a democracy. The two clerics looked up as the bishop closed a folder in front of him, a rather fat folder.

"Good afternoon, Monsignor," the bishop said as he rose and extended his hand. The rise from his seat nowhere neared his rise in the ranks. "Obviously I got your letter and thought we should get together." Father Quigley also rose, shuffled some notes into a pile, swept the pile into a briefcase and awaited his turn to shake Monsignor's hand. Then the bishop turned to him and said, "OK, Mark. That's it for now. I'll call you later." The reply was equally informal, "Thanks, Bishop. Until later."

After Father Quigley had quit the room, the bishop gave his full attention to the standing Monsignor. "Please sit down, Monsignor. Sorry I'm running a bit late today."

That's good, Monsignor thought. Have him apologetic at the beginning and then be gracious. "Of course I understand, Your Excellency. We all have those days." He hoped that he sounded more gracious than patronizing, but he couldn't be sure and decided to wait until This One had showed his hand. But it didn't happen the way it was played out in the waiting room. The bishop waited until Monsignor was seated and then walked over to his window. It was a short walk and seemed to take forever. Monsignor thought he was going to leave the room, but the bishop just pushed the drapes aside with one hand and stared out on the tree tops that were almost level with the window. He said nothing, just stared for a moment, drew in a deep breath and said, without turning around, "Monsignor, how do you understand the words, 'The truth will set you free'?"

Monsignor was stunned. He knew the line was from Shakespeare although he could not recall the play. Besides, this was not why he was here, to engage in some sort of a game. Before he could respond, the bishop had turned around and looked at him; he seemed not to have expected an answer. He returned to his chair, sat down and put his hands, rather protectively Monsignor thought, on the folder in front of him. The folder itself did not surprise Monsignor. After all, if Father Wycek were to go to another parish, This One would have to have all the documents handy, the recommendations, the reports from the seminary—everything, in fact, which would allow him to be placed in a suitable situation, one which help him grow into ecclesiastical usefulness.

The bishop opened the file and said, "You've been ordained for thirty-two years this May, haven't you?" My God! It's my dossier, not Wycek's! Monsignor thought. What is he doing with my file? And then, of course it dawned on him; this was a preliminary interview before This One sent in his name to the Apostolic Delegate for nomination. The business with the Wycek creature was secondary. He almost laughed but outwardly he remained calm and reserved, just the way he knew he would be expected to act when the investigation had been completed, the nomination announced, and the consecration behind him.

"Yes, Your Excellency. Thirty-two years on May

19th." That was a good length of time. Just right, in fact: long enough to have wisdom and experience, short enough to have years ahead of him to exercise those virtues. His voice did not say, "Just think of that!" but his tone managed to convey it.

"Thirty-two years," the bishop repeated more slowly than Monsignor would have liked. It sounded more like a regret than a compliment. "And in that time you have had several associates." So it was about Wycek after all. Then why is my file there? "Each time you have requested a change of associate, your request has been honored. In those thirty-two years you certainly have done fine things for the diocese. Yes, fine things, indeed. And of course, the diocese is grateful to you." No, it is not about Wycek at all; it is the investigation for the Delegate. Monsignor was getting confused. He had better wait until the game plan was clearer before he committed himself on anything specific.

"That's one of the truths we have to work with, Monsignor. Your long years of service." Pause. "Another truth is the letter you sent me this week, requesting the removal of Father Wycek." He opened the file and slipped the letter off the top of the papers and closed the file again. "'Father Wycek is unsuitable'," he read. "'"...for the good of the Church...' And that, Monsignor, is one of your truths." (Monsignor wished he could remember the play the bishop's quote came from; it might give him a clue to what was going on.) "But we have other truths that also have to be considered."

The bishop paused, looked down at the closed file, laid Monsignor's letter on top of the file, and then like one who has made a difficult decision from which there is no turning back, said, "Seldom are truths pleasant, Monsignor. Each one of us wants to be thought of as a truthful person and be admired for it. We call Satan the Father of Lies for good reason because we avoid the truth with silence until the

117

silence itself becomes another lie. And when we speak, we pretend we are telling the truth. In reality, we are only gossiping.

"But there is another kind of silence which is the truth, or at least reveals the truth more eloquently than any speech could possibly reveal. It is always difficult to know which the silence is until later: Is it truth or a lie? We ask ourselves. Frequently we just forget the incident and go on to something else. At other times, we have to act on that silence and pray fervently that it is the silence of truth.

"You have a right to the truth. You will find pain in it but I hope you will also find freedom in it. Last year when I talked to the ordination class about their assignments, your name came up. We had five young men, all eager and full of excitement over their first appointments. They acted like I could send them to the moon with the scratch of my pen and they would have been happy for the journey. When I asked them about Saint Andrew's, there was a silence which was no lie this time but the truth. And it was simply this: no one wanted to be assigned to your parish. When I asked them if there was some problem, they just looked at each otherlike some guilty conspirators. They had obviously discussed the possibility among themselves before that. But still they said nothing. A nervousness seemed to arise among them which was unmistakable, and they did not need to say anything else. Because I knew. I knew by their silence what they could not say. Your reputation for chewing up associates has infiltrated the seminary.

"Finally, Father Wycek spoke. He said that he would accept the assignment, and he said it simply and without elaboration. Just, 'I will be willing to go there, Bishop.' The others looked at him but they added nothing more. I asked him if he was sure, and he said yes. Again, just a few words in all simplicity. But I knew what they cost him. So I told him, 'Try it for a year, or even six months. If it proves unbearable, just let me know and we'll do something.'

"And so, Monsignor, I have kept you imprisoned in a lie by my silence. I knew of your reputation and said nothing when I should have called you in long ago and talked to you. But, just like everyone else, I hoped that you would change on your own, and the unpleasantness could be avoided.

"That's why I was not surprised to receive a letter from Saint Andrew's, although I thought it would be from him and not you. In the eight months he has been there, I have never heard a word of complaint. I have gotten several letters from parishioners praising his homilies and thanking me for sending him there, but from him I have heard nothing.

"So, Monsignor, I will transfer him as you requested but I will not be sending anyone else there. But just to keep truth on the table, you should know the other options. I could transfer you and leave him there to help the new pastor, or I could ask you to take early retirement. Mark thought it would be best for you to just stay there. He even made a few suggestions for a replacement for Father Wycek, but I just cannot spare anyone else right now nor can I in good conscience ask anyone else to go there.

"I know this comes as a blow, but it is the truth we both have to face. It's a new world, Monsignor, since the days when we were in the seminary and when we were ordained. A lot has happened and continues to happen. We may not like the changes that are thrust upon us, but we cannot ignore them either.

"And now you can be truly free because you have the bitterness of truth exposed. You are free to grow and change, and you are equally free to remain adamant in remaining the way you are. But now, at least, the choice is yours."

Monsignor sat there numb. His mind was fighting the words he was hearing. It was not supposed to be this way.

He came to discuss the unsuitableness of Father Wycek and here he was being lectured to about not being appreciated in the diocese. He deserved a curate who understood what he could offer, one who would be tractable and pliant and who would eventually be a fit pastor in the diocese. He felt contempt for This One who would let the newly ordained push him around like that. But he said nothing, just looked blankly and tried to convey attention to what was being said without registering his revulsion for such ingratitude. He let Father Wycek become a blank spot in his mind; there would be time to deal with him later.

"When Pilate asked Jesus what truth was, he got no answer. Maybe there is no answer and there are only facts. And maybe Jesus' silence was itself the ultimate truth. But sometimes facts and truth are the same, I suspect," the bishop continued. He sounded sad that such should be the case. But then he added his silence to the silence of the cosmos.

"I'm truly sorry, Monsignor. There are times when I despise this office." Monsignor was not sure if he meant the room or the position, but the comment only added confusion to his bewilderment.

Outside, a car horn honked and a child's voice was heard, "Throw it over here." And then nothing more.

Monsignor did not trust his voice as he rose. He would show This One how a misunderstood martyr took adversity. He bowed toward the seated bishop, just his head and only slightly, not his back. He squared his shoulders, turned and left the room. By the time he reached the elevator, he decided that the Peter's Pence Collection would be down by thirty percent next year; and by the time he reached his car, he knew that there would be boiled chicken (which he knew the bishop hated) at the Confirmation dinner. If it was the truth This One wanted, by God! He was going to get it.

Shared Responsibility

Thursday night! Damn!

If St. Peter were to ask if he wanted a root canal without Novocain, or open heart surgery through his left thigh, or shoot the Colorado River without a life preserver, or a Thursday night parish Council meeting before he could be let out of purgatory, he would be hard pressed to choose. But his teeth were fine, his heart pumped predictably, and he knew how to swim. So perhaps his multiple choices weren't all that bad. He hoped he might have an emergency hospital call, or quite possibly an unannounced visit from the bishop, or a call from the pope, asking his thoughts on birth control — anything, in fact, that would preserve him from the need for showing up at the monthly bickering session called "Shared Responsibility After Vatican Two", or in the words of the parish bulletin, "Monthly Parish Council Meeting", Thursday evening at 7:30 p.m.

Damn!

The Council's president was, to use safe words acceptable in mixed company, a Nice Man. Making decisions, even in his home life, had never been his strongest suit. An overwhelming desire to keep the peace, to have friendly conversations, to be liked by one and all had been his M.O. since his earliest childhood days. It had worked so far and he expected that it would work until the vast throng attended his funeral since he was such a Nice Man.

The Council's secretary kept meticulous notes. Every thought, every suggestion, every belch and hiccup made its way into the minutes. Reading those minutes was like reliving the whole, hideous, ghastly experience, or like having one's whole life flash before a drowning man's eyes. But efficient? The word was invented for her and she was the archetype of efficiency. Even though it was at the cost of a sense of humor or gentleness, she was efficient. She could produce, at a three second notice, all the notes, minutes, reports, and files that had been accumulated in the parish in the past 23 years. Without judgment or priorities, the whole of an ecclesiastical world was at her fingertips. It was comforting and threatening at the same time.

And there were the Mainstays, those who knew how to maneuver their way onto the Council through coercion, manipulation, intimidation, or pity. They were the real danger. They were the ones who knew what a parish was and how to keep it that way ever since the dear Fr. Martin had built the church, erected the still-present statues and decreed that Eden had once again been created on our earth and nothing could alter it. To them, Council meetings were simply ways of keeping his memory alive and rededicating the parish to his ideals and vision.

Thursday night! Damn!

Father Benson got his soul together, practiced the little Zen he remembered from one of the priests' retreats, put blank paper and a leaky ball-point pen into his attaché case, and walked over to the parish hall. Even walking into the hall was test of his dedication and heroic virtue. It had been built by Dear Father Martin and could be used for nothing other than what he had planned. The teenage dances were, of course, out of place. Lock-ins for young people's retreats were suspect but could be used for such a purpose if a policeman were hired for the evening. A parish party with wine and cheese was borderline because everyone knew how wine and cheese parties could get out of hand and would not be fitting in a parish hall and who knew what else it could lead to? If the mere presence of the hall was not depressing to Father Benson, it certainly was not exciting.

The Mainstays arrived first. That was one of their functions and duties. For it must be noted who was eager to participate and who was sluggish in arrival. After all, re-elections would be coming up soon and these things should be noted and broadcast. Father Martin was, after all, the very model of punctuality and his spirit was enshrined by those who worshipped there.

After the Mainstays came the Necessaries. These were the people who found themselves appointed or elected to the Council when they were on vacation or out of town. But they were on other committees of the parish and would therefore have to be there to give their reports and findings. Therefore, quite obviously, they had to be on the Council itself. It was their duty.

In deference to Father Martin, Father Benson felt it his solemn obligation to be at least three minutes late. He was inured to the stares and silent judgment from the Mainstays who looked at him with scarcely concealed disdain. "Let them look all they want," he told himself. "I have a bottle of Cuddy Sark waiting to be opened after this fiasco is over." And there was still the possibility that he would get that call from the hospital or the pope.

Mainstay One nodded to the president who responded with, "Well, now that we are all here, shall we begin?" Father Benson looked at Mainstay One and at her content that she had put the operation into motion. Her husband had had the good fortune to die after a mere seven years of marriage and she had taken his absence out on the parish. The parish had become her husband, her lover, her employer, and the brunt of her energies ever since. The pastors between Father Martin and Father Benson had called her, with some justification, 'Bishop Betty' and she gloried in the title. Father Benson however, called her

124

nothing but Elizabeth and then only when it was necessary to speak to her.

And so they began. The president looked at the members of the Council and asked, "Who would like to lead us in prayer?" No one ever did and so they all looked at Father Benson. What were they paying him for if not to pray? Because it was easier to say a few words addressed to the God of Wisdom and Discernment than to sit there and listen to someone else, usually Mainstay Three, invoke the divinity's attendance on several of her favorite issues which she would reveal in due course. Father Benson said a standard Come, Holy Spirit, and they got on with the business at hand.

First came the secretary's question, "Has everyone got their minutes?" There was a rustling of papers, shifting of seats, and several noddings of heads. Yes, everyone had "their" minutes.

From the president: "Are there any amendments or corrections?" Several of the members then began to read their minutes for the first time.

"Didn't we decide that Russ Larson would get an estimate on putting new sod on the northeast corner of the church? I don't see anything about that here." The question came from Bill Checkers, who was absent at the last meeting.

Mainstay One cleared her throat and informed him, "You weren't here when we decided that it would cost too much to sod the northeast corner, especially when we need the money to repaint the shrine." She then sat back, having reestablished her position of chief speaker for all things historical. The president nodded and if his nod could have had speech would have said, "That's just what we did. We surely did."

"Anything else?" the president asked.

Bishop Betty looked around, daring anyone to make corrections or amendments, or even to ask questions as had

Russ. After all, she had taken a hand in preparing the minutes and therefore she knew them to be without flaw.

From the president: "Then we'll accept the minutes as read." The minutes had not been read but he had heard the phrase somewhere and it sounded official and he wanted to be seen as competent and official. "Now we'll have the reports."

Father Benson hated reports with a hatred usually reserved for bounced checks in the Sunday collection and mortal sin. Every detail of every report was gone over with the same dedication and fervor with which our forefathers shaped the Constitution: idea by idea, line by line, syllable by syllable. If Fred Lasky, head of the Building Committee, had been asked to check on the broken windows in the rectory, he would have given the estimates or actual costs from each of the hardware stores, each of the building contractors, and each of the garage sales he had investigated. He would have bought nothing, but the costs were all there for all to see and discuss.

At this point Mainstay One would usually opine that nothing need be done yet because Sears would be having its annual sale in three weeks and she heard that window panes would be on special. Fred then would neatly stack his notes and papers together and bind them together with a paper clip and wait for the next item. He figured he was entitled to only one topic since he had been bested by the best with sodding the corner of the church. Besides, he was quite content to vote with the majority.

Father Benson figured Fred's motto in life was 'Don't make waves and you won't drown in the bathtub.'

"Well, we do have that open position on the Council." Marion Shepherd had moved out of the state several months before and now it was time to get a replacement. The usual grace-filled process had been observed, which meant that over a beer or during the conversation after one of the Sunday Masses, the president had casually asked someone — in this case Ted Harmon — if he would like to be on the Council. Ted was safe and that counted for much in the ways the Holy Spirit could work in developing new membership. "Ted Harmon has said he would serve and I think we ought to elect him."

Father Benson could not resist, "And how many others were asked about it? How about those who have taken the diocesan leadership courses? Were they given any consideration?"

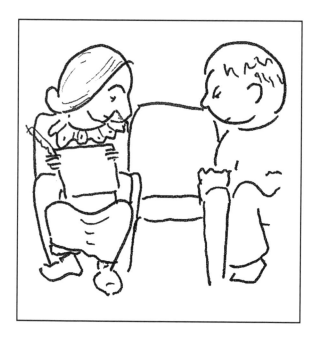

An embarrassed silence followed. Challenges were not the stuff of dreams for the Mainstays. Dangerous, they thought them. Mainstay One said, "It's very difficult to get people to serve on the Council." She had been on the Council even before the days of Dear Father Martin and was honestly puzzled that others could not be as dedicated as she to the cause of the parish.

Her statement hung in the air like so many plucked

chickens in an open air market. Even the president was made uncomfortable. The secretary quickly looked at the agenda and said, "We still need to decide about the Christmas decorations."

Irmalene Hoffstetter, who had been on the Council for the past three meetings and was still a bit unsure of when to introduce topics and when to vote said, "I had someone ask me about the CCD classes and why we stopped during the summer. They—," she was not about to give away her sources, "—said that religion does not stop and learning shouldn't either."

Now Mainstay Two was on firm ground. Education was her forte. In fact, if education was a symphony she would have played conductor, flute and violin sections alone, and still have energy left for the timpani. As a teacher, she had not been privy to the reaction of her students who — to a boy or girl — considered her cruel and inadequate. "Teachers need time off too and that's what summer's for."

Irmalene look puzzled and waited for the rest of the barrage. It didn't come, for as far as Mainstay Two was concerned, there was nothing more to say. And so there the matter rested.

The president looked timidly around the table and asked, "Are there any reports? Finance?" This set the whole Council off on a frenzy of activity. Yes, by God! There were reports. So the shuffling of papers and the rustling of shifting hams in the seats filled the room.

"I've noticed that collections are down—again," Mainstay One, Keeper of All Things Financial and Spiritual, shot into the hen house. Everyone looked at Father Benson, who consistently refused to preach about those who are not giving enough to the church. This was a favorite game in which no opinion was left unspoken. The high watermark for comparison was the boom days of oilrigs in the pastures, which coincidentally marked the last days of Dear Father Martin. Stores had closed, shops had gone out of business, and homes had been vacated and left unsold. But all that meant little since it was the pastor's responsibility to preach many a time and oft on the need for the others to give so that they could have 'a comfortable nest egg for the church.'

Father Benson wondered what a 'comfortable nest egg' would look like. He had visions of an emu sitting on the president's bald head, waiting for something to hatch. During this revere, the flood gates opened and he could hear comments which had not been made since last month when the financial report was given. "We all need to accept our responsibility," said Mainstay One as she looked at him. "We've been spending..." Father Benson drifted back to the emu and wondered what Mainstay One would look like as an animal. Surely she darted around like a ferret, but she had the bulk of a badger. And there was something in the eyes that suggested a pit viper.

"Not a pleasant bit of business," thought Father Benson. The word 'harridan' came to mind, but he could not remember the exact definition so he let it go.

The next fifteen minutes were dedicated, like so much blood on an Inca altar, to the need to conserve money and watch how much they were spending. Having exhausted the topic, although the idea of rearranging the priorities never occurred to anyone, there was a satisfied silence. Again the president asked as he looked at the agenda which had not changed since the days of Dear Father Martin, "Are there are any other reports?"

The Women's Club of Saint Veronica report was next. Every month, on the third Sunday without fail, lukewarm coffee and stale buns ("They are cheaper if you buy two-day old buns") were served between the two Sunday Masses. The women all collected in the kitchen and rehashed the latest gossip and found out what high school girl "was in trouble," what upstart boys had overturned garbage cans, what divorcée had gone to communion, who had not put an envelope in the collection, and whose children were laughing in church. There was no bit of naughtiness which was left untouched. The men stayed in the hall during these expressions of "the women's ministry." There the conversation stuck pretty much to hunting out of season, the weather, preparations for spring planting, the job market, and how good it was that the pope wouldn't let women be ordained.

So the Women's Club of Saint Veronica had much to report. "We served four gallons of coffee and seven dozen buns last month," said the Club's president. "I think we have to do something about all the children who get in line before the adults have a chance to get a bun, and some of the children are taking two before anyone else has had a chance to get one." The next five minutes were filled with ideas like having one of the children's fathers police the line; maybe we could hand the buns out instead of letting the children just grab; perhaps it would be a good idea to hide the buns until the children have been through; how about a sign indicating which were the children's buns and which were the adult's buns?

Nothing was resolved and there were no motions to second, so the meeting continued. Father Benson looked at the president, but all he could see was the Cuddy Sark in his cabinet. His thirst was mounting and he knew there were topics yet to parade before the Council. There was still nothing said about the color of the shed which had not yet been built. But it was certainly good to plan ahead.

"Has anyone noticed that the light bulb is out in the east side of the church?" Again a cold silence fell over the group as one of the guests spoke up. Everyone had noticed the deficiency and they all wondered when the maintenance committee would get together to change it. To call attention to this lapse was considered to be in very bad taste since the Council could certainly oversee its own house without outside interference. They were all too polite to call it to the attention of the representative on the Council. So Mainstay One said, "I'm sure it will be taken care of, Dear." And so there the matter rested.

"Liturgy?"

The liturgy committee was activated only in times of high liturgical season, namely Lent and Advent, and was pretty well circumscribed by the decorations and the music. Freida Willums, liturgy's representative, had played the organ for several years now and had her standard opening line ready, "I wish we could get someone else to play the organ on Sundays." Three times in as many years there had been volunteers to play the organ and each one had been dismissed with Freida's "Thanks, but Dear, you don't play fast/slow/loud/soft enough for the congregation. But we will certainly use you if we get in a pinch. These people certainly are difficult to play for, so you had better let me take care of it for now." Still, at the Council meeting, everyone was reminded of the generous service performed at each of the Sunday Masses by our harried musician. Decorations were not an entirely different matter since the wreaths bought by Dear Father Martin were still used at Christmas and the purple ribbons during Lent.

"They are still serviceable and we don't want to waste money, now do we?" Mainstay One said. At this meeting, however, the announcement that it would be nice to have another Sunday organist was allowed to stand on its own and there were the usual appreciative gentle shakings of the heads, as though to say, "Golly, Freida, we wish we could help you, but you know how it is." And since Freida knew how it was and how it had better be, they moved on. But Freida was not quite finished with her business. "I'm having trouble teaching the people a new Gloria."

David Hartesty's chief claim to parochial fame was that he was never known to have opened his mouth to sing a note, not even bits and dabs of Silent Night, said, "Well, Freida, you've got to teach them the new stuff so we don't keep going back the old stuff all the time."

Now Freida was on very solid ground. Father Benson looked at his watch and knew this would take approximately ten minutes, so he drifted off into a brown study which included death by hanging, death on the highway, death by accidental electrocution, and death by fire. He figured that any of The Four Last Things would keep his mind off the bottle back at the rectory. He heard, out of the corner of his ear, "...so if the people would come fifteen minutes early every Sunday we could teach them..." and he drifted off again. The vision of a whole community coming to church fifteen minutes early to learn new hymns was more than he was prepared to entertain.

"Anything from the Funeral Committee?" This was the happy group that gathered like a bunch of vultures at the first hint of serious illness. A whole Sophoclean drama would be played out with meticulous attention to detail and pathos. Father Benson remembered with incredible clarity when Mainstay Two's husband died. He was standing close to the coffin — where else? — looking at the flowers for want of anything better to do. The people seemed to appreciate it when he just stood there, as though lost in the thought of happier days and blissful memories of the dearly departed. Actually, he was trying to remember the name of the dead person for the next day's funeral, but he confided that reality to no one. At the wake, Mainstay One had come in on angel wings behind him and had said to Mainstay Two, "You are doing beautifully, Dear."

"Am I doing beautifully, really?"

"Yes, you are doing beautifully."

Father Benson had wanted to change places with the corpse. That or just throw up. Actually he did neither, but whenever the Funeral Committee report came in he felt that he should be congratulated for doing beautifully when he didn't shriek like a banshee in heat.

Since no one had died since the last Council meeting, there was nothing to report. The committee's representative, Latitia Rawlings, however, could not let silence be her guide and just because there had been no funeral to dwell on in all its details, she did want it in the next minutes and said, "We are running low on baking soda for the Funeral Committee and we won't be able to bake any fresh bread." And there was not a person in the county who was not aware of Latitia's pride in baking bread. Some of her less successful efforts had been used as anchors on fishing boats; others were immortalized as door stops. But Latitia's bread was always remarked on and noted, and she could be relied on to bake "a little something" for a funeral. Therefore the seeming innocence of no baking soda could not be taken lightly and would have to come to the entire Council's attention.

Father Benson, to show his attention and authority, said, "Get some and we'll take it out of petty cash." This did not please the Finance Committee, but no one was prepared to make an issue out of it.

Father Benson rather pointedly looked at his watch. Three minutes and seventeen seconds to go. The president got the hint and asked if there were any further business. They all stared at Father Benson as though he were expected to launch into some grand and engrossing scheme for the future of the parish, or ask their advice about getting a new roof for the rectory, or announce that from now on we would take up a second collection for the nest egg, or something like get an assistant who would really understand their concerns as Dear Father Martin did. But there was nothing.

The president asked if anyone wanted to close the meeting with a prayer. No one did so they all again looked at Father Benson. The only thing he could think of was "thank you, God, for being with us in times of tribulation" but figured this would not go unnoticed, so instead he lead a very hasty Our Father and dashed back to the rectory. Standing around making small talk was one of his least accomplishments.

One minute and seven seconds after the final Amen, he was seated in his armchair, three fingers of Cuddy Sark in his glass and a look of sheer relaxation on his face. "Thank God," he thought, "they did not bring up who is supposed to get the Christmas collection."

Mother and the Studebaker

It is only because you have pressed me that I now relate the story of Mother and the Studebaker. There are some things I have always believed, that should be kept in the dark confines of memory or misbegotten myth, not thrust into the light of rational scrutiny. And few of Mother's actions were capable of rationality or scrutiny. It would be comforting if I could see Mother as marching to a different drummer, but that would be misleading and quite possibly, a lie.

Mother first of all did not march; she galumphed with panache in all directions at once, deciding on her destination only when she arrived. And then there was the air of triumph that she had come to what was obviously the object of her trek. It might be a grocery store (although she despised cooking), a florist (although she hated dead flowers), or a gas station (although she had nothing but a holy hatred for gas fumes). Destination was irrelevant. Purpose was all.

As for the marching song that heralded Mother's step, only the Song of the Spheres could accompany her gait and match the glint in her eye. It was not only a different

135

drummer; it was an entirely different orchestra which could confuse the 1812 with the William Tell Overtures that had a sporting chance. And even then, it was less than even money.

I was constantly torn between delight in watching clerks, salesmen, and attendants thrown into utter and unalleviated confusion on one side, and on the other in embarrassment when I would be called upon to witness to the justice of her cause. And I never knew which it would be nor why. I was particularly bewildered when we met one of my friends or my friend's mothers in one of the shops because I just knew there would be what we called "a scene." A scene could be anything from a mild exchange of banalities to a confrontation of Homeric proportions. The first could occur if my friend merely had a dirty face, the latter if I were aced out of the spelling contest by some obscure word, known only to my teacher and Webster.

Meetings between Mother and any of my teachers were always epic. They were simply proof of the adage about winning the battle and losing the war because I knew that I had to face the teacher the next day and the only weapon in my arsenal would be a muted threat that Mother would come and have another conference. It was usually more than enough.

I do not remember being a fearful child but I must have lived my entire childhood in constant terror and as I said, quite obviously there are some things which should be forgotten.

But I digress. I wanted to tell you the story of Mother and the Studebaker. Perhaps there will be some kernel of comfort to be found within, some note of encouragement to continue fighting the good fight, or some memory that needs further atonement. I cannot be sure. I know only that I have been so traumatized that every time I have to buy a new car I spend sleepless nights, and when I do doze off I awake with sweaty palms and throbbing head.

Well you might ask, "Why a Studebaker?" This is just another of Mother's multifaceted virtues, for she was loyal if nothing else. We had been driving a Studebaker for years and she was convinced of the dependability of the machine, provided of course that it behaved itself. There was the time in the old Studebaker when she broke the axle going through sands dunes — that is another story for another time — but forced the car into submission for another three hundred miles of extraordinary noises, which she explained away as there being a tree dragging behind us. Since there was no tree branch dragging behind us, it meant that it must be wedged under the car somewhere and we shouldn't worry about it. The noise was cold comfort to this reassurance. The axle was fixed only when we stalled on the train tracks at Fifth Avenue during rush hour and when a train was coming— but that too is another story and I have only a fleeting and sketchy memory of the terror in the mechanic's face when he told Mother that the axle was not under warranty. To Mother, an automobile should be as endurable as an Egyptian pyramid and as thrifty with gas as a skate board. So when the time came for the old Studebaker to be laid to rest from sheer exhaustion, it was time to seek a worthy replacement, although in 1940 they did not make cars the way they used to.

I already told you that Mother was loyal. There was no question of considering other models. Buicks, Fords, and Dodges were not in the same league simply because Mother had never driven a Buick, a Ford, or a Dodge. To her, comparison-shopping was for the indecisive and faint of heart and neither were admirable qualities to her, and they presented the types of people who had to be taught a lesson "for their own good."

You will notice that I have not mentioned Father in this, and this is for a very good reason: Father was tolerant, decisive, and had a superb (if somewhat strange) sense of humor. He found early in their marriage that he need not play Young Lochinvar to Mother's Clinging Maiden. His assertion of authority was not diminished because he knew when to hold his tongue and when to have the final word. Mother would have had no chance of intimidating the car salesman if Father had not decided that a new car was on the family agenda. He took care of the broader picture and let Mother fill in the trivial details, like the make, model, and color.

The demise of the old Studebaker was sudden and unexpected to everyone, except perhaps the Studebaker. There was no final assault from a sideswiping street car on the icy streets of Chicago (that did not come until later and then it was with the new car); there was no unloosening of bolts that made conversation in the car impossible; there was no consumptive coughing of the engine to warn of impending non-functionality. Quite simply, one day in its own great good time, the car refused to budge. No amount of cajoling, turning the starter, or pushing back and forth and bouncing up and down from the driver's seat on Mother's part (although this had worked on several occasions) could coax the car into activity. It was very much like the stories I had heard from childhood about Grandmother deciding that she had lived long enough; she turned her eyes to her God, fixed an inscrutable smile on her face, and expired. Now that I consider it, maybe there might be something genetic in our family— but that is too scary to think about now and I can handle only one tale of terror at a time and I wanted to tell you about buying the Studebaker.

One day at breakfast, Father opined that since the car was sitting dead in the driveway, perhaps it was time to get a new car. Now breakfasts were rather casual affairs. We came down to the kitchen in the same order that we got into the bathroom. And they were rather early meals since Mother believed with her whole heart and soul that anyone who slept after 6:00 am was obviously in mortal sin. She

138

herself was a virtuous early riser, so she knew the truth of her belief with the same assurance the early martyrs had when they faced Caligula on some bright morning when the beasts had not been fed for ten days.

We were asked the inevitable question if we wanted pancakes or not. I have already mentioned that Mother was not the Julia Childs of pre-war days, although her pancakes were the envy of many a retread factory. There was just something about following the Betty Crocker directions which bored Mother. The print on the box was small and Mother's interest in taking directions even smaller. One day the proportions for our pancakes would be one box of flour to one cup of water. Another time it would be—depending on the weather, the stars or Mother's intuition—four cups of water to one-half cup of flour. Early in our lives, we had learned that corn flakes would always be the safest. Mother knew this too, but at least she had created the illusion that we were being well fed on what we asked for.

But on this particular morning Father said, yes he would like some pancakes. We all dropped our spoons into our cereal bowls with a clatter that could not have been mistaken for anything other than the shock it betrayed. We children looked at each other, hoping for some sign of the significance of this portent. We were at a loss, but so was Mother—but only at first. She could not believe her ears: someone had actually wanted pancakes, and not just any pancakes but her pancakes. We cast our eyes down and refused to pick up our spoons because we did not want to miss a single syllable of what we knew would be revealed.

It was a bit like Zachariah being struck dumb when he doubted that he would beget a man-child. I said that only at first was Mother speechless. In a trice she had yanked open the cupboard and announced, "Whoops, sorry. We don't have any flour." Mother was used to having the reward for having offered to make the pancakes and the joy of not having to do it; besides that, Mother was seldom sorry. To both Mother's and Father's credit, neither expected anything different and the mood had been set for what was to come.

It was Father who broke the tension, as we knew it would be since he had been the one to reject the ritual. "I think it's time," he said, "to get a new car." Those nine words, quietly spoken and without emphasis, initiated the chain of events which in later years would be known as Mother and the Studebaker. I understand that on his deathbed the salesman was heard to mutter, "Please don't let that woman in here." But that is only hearsay and I cannot tell you anymore than what I have seen with my own eyes and heard with my own ears. I do know for a fact, however, that he left the Studebaker dealership within hours after we got a new car.

Now Mother had a special hat that she wore for solemn occasions, like parent-teacher meetings, Midnight Mass at Christmas, and funerals. It fit tightly on her head, much like a skull cap. But there the resemblance ended. There were feathers; large, fluffy, eye-gouging feathers. They were firmly jabbed into the hat at mid-point and branched out in both directions from her face. People in front of her were safe, as were those who kept a respectful distance behind. It was only those on either side who were in mortal danger. More than one unsuspecting friend or acquaintance would leave off talking to Mother to tend the lacerations on cheek or forehead.

It was always a pleasure to watch Mother use her hat to claim her space. I was perfectly safe however, since I was not tall enough to intercept her 180-degree horizon sweeps. Only once when we were sitting side by side in church did I get jabbed. Afterwards the doctor said that my eardrum had not been permanently damaged. It is important that you have some idea of Mother's hat because it plays a small but rather meaningful part in the purchase of the Studebaker.

And it was this very hat which she wore on that particular Saturday when Father asked for pancakes.

Since the old Studebaker was lifeless and limp in the driveway, I do not remember how we got to the showroom. I do remember something about a phone call and the expectation that we would be picked up and delivered with the greatest possible speed. But whether it was the cab company or the showroom I cannot recall. Since Father sat in the front seat, and as long as Mother sat in the back with me and did not turn her head and look out the window, the driver was safe. That, I do remember. Memory fails me however, on where my siblings were. When I look back on that day, it seems to me that they were both incredibly busy and could not partake in the venture. It amazes me even to this day that they could have been so wise while still in their tender years.

I remember nothing special about the showroom. There were probably three or four cars on the floor. Glistening, sleek, burnished they sat, like mechanical gods waiting the obeisance of the worshipping faithful. When Mother saw them, a strange look came into her eyes. I can compare it only to the look that must have been in a grave robber's eyes when he first came upon a long-buried Mayan treasure. Words were superfluous and would have only destroyed the magic of the moment as Mother stood amid the reflecting surfaces of those new cars.

Father walked over to a rather sedate black model, cocked his head to one side, obviously appraising it. He raised an eyebrow, which could easily be interpreted as "This one will be fine." He looked over at Mother whose look had changed from avarice to disbelief. She drew in a long breath which straightened her back and slightly arched her neck. The silence spoke volumes. And by that look, she signaled that Father had brought us here, but what we did here was her domain. Majestically she turned toward the gray, four-door model, nodded with the merest inclination, much like Queen Victoria nodding to Gladstone that he might speak. And the choice had been made in all the simplicity.

The salesman was quite obviously pleased that a sale had been made with such little fuss and haggling. Little did he know and nothing he could guess what was in store. He had mentally counted his commission and thought he might even be able to knock off for the rest of the day. He went into the manager, spoke a few muttered words, returned to us and said, "The manager will talk to you about the financing," the smile still pasted upon his lips. It was that pleasant smile which his family would recall whenever they remembered him in later years because it was quite possibly the last smile he would ever wear. He may have counted on his commission. He did not count on Mother demanding a test drive.

Now a doomed man is offered a final meal of his choice, a cigarette or two, perhaps a last phone call, or a hearty "what-ho!" from the warden as he leaves his cell for the last time. Count that man as blessed who finds he is merely bankrupted, or that his cancer is only mildly painful but inoperable; or consider the jolly fellow who found that the last life boat had left the Titanic, or Joseph as he was lowered by his brothers into the well for some future sale. Compare them, I ask you, to the salesman who contemplated an effortless agreement on a four-door gray Studebaker on this one Saturday morning and you will have some idea of the ambiance in that showroom.

For those of you accustomed to automatic transmissions, I must pause for a moment to describe the mechanics of a four-on-the-wheel transmission. For, you see, it was a new thing with the 1940 gray Studebaker under discussion. The old Studebaker had a no-nonsense cane-sized shift on the floor, right there between the driver and the passenger. One need only drop one's hand from the steering wheel, grab the knob — usually about the size of a

142

baseball — swing the whole shoulder some forty-five degrees, and pull down. That was first. Second gear was a beautifully symmetric H: Grab the knob, push the shift to neutral, swing the stick to the right, and quickly thrust up. For third gear, one merely grabbed the knob and pulled — past neutral and down as far as the shift would go.

Did I mention the clutch? Along with the acrobatics of propelling the lever to its various destinations, one had to engage the clutch. Now the clutch was a floor pedal, to the left of the brake and roughly the same size as the brake. In fact, it was distinguished only by the result of being depressed. If you simply sat, idle and expectant, then you had pushed in the clutch. If you came to a screeching halt in the middle of the street, you had pushed the brake. Since we are involved in these transactions, I think I should mention that the gas pedal was flat, the one closest to the shift lever and was at the mercy of the right foot only. The clutch was engaged only by the left foot. Most people thought of the brake as part of the right foot's responsibility because one would not engage both gas and brake at the same time. No, no. The brake and the clutch, yes. The gas and the brake together? Never.

Well, hardly ever. Mother had developed her own unique way of shifting. She would push in the clutch, put the transmission into neutral, release the clutch, and then step on both the brake and the gas at the same time. Her reasoning had the stunning simplicity of one of the Holy Innocents who did not bother to wake up for the carnage. By depressing both the brake and the gas at the same time, she deduced both feet could be happily utilized and the engine would not stall in the winter. It would keep the heater operating as an added bonus. Further, the automobile would stop. To her, it was clear, clean Aristotelian logic unfettered by any Platonic overlays of the good, the true, or the beautiful. I should also add that early in her driving career, Mother had learned to down-shift and save the brake for some future emergency. Occasionally at a stop sign it might be a near thing, but until now had posed no particular problem — at least for the family.

The Studebaker in question had, for that year's model, moved the shift from the floor to the steering wheel. No longer need one reach down to shift: now one merely extended the hand, and like one drying nail polish or shooing flies, flick the wrist and shift gears. Mother wore her hat and was used to a floor shift. That's all you need to know about the test drive. The salesman was ignorant of Mother's proclivities and could see the hat coming and so felt no danger in agreeing to "take the little lady for a spin."

Father and the manager were occupied signing papers, transferring titles, negotiating floor pads and otherwise doing their male-bonding thing as Mother got into the driver's seat.   The salesman moved gracefully into the passenger's seat and I sat in the back.

No car in the world has ever had its starter under the clutch. The old Studebaker did not, the ads for various new models never mentioned it, and no one in Detroit would have countenanced it. But the builders and designers of the 1940 Studebaker did. Mother had the key in her right hand, saw the slot for it, and then scanned the dashboard for the starter. It wasn't by the speedometer, it wasn't by the gas gauge, and it wasn't by the temperature indicator. She pointed with the forefinger of her left hand, always game for a new venture, but the starter was not by the hand brake, nor by the light switch, nor even by the windshield wiper. The salesman emitted a tiny chortle as if to say, "Gottcha on that, little lady." Aloud he said, "It's under the clutch."

Mother looked disdainfully at the pedal in question, and then tilted her head to include the little button under it. As one who knows who is the master of her fate and guardian of her soul, she jumped on the starter around the clutch with all the art and skill of a Judith taking command of Holofernes's head. But she didn't depress the clutch and

144

the car was still in reverse. With a rather violent leap the whole car, including its passengers, gave a lurch a good six inches into the air, and shot backwards as it came to rest on the side of Father's first choice of a black sedan.

Now Mother was nothing if not a quick study in comprehending a new situation and she knew that something was awry, so she lifted her foot from the starter button. By now, both the car and the salesmen were cowed into subjectivity and Mother was not entirely displeased with the result. He did suggest, and to his credit it was with perfect humility and mindfulness, that perhaps she would like him to take the car out onto the street to begin the test drive. Mother allowed it, as that would be acceptable and got out of the car. He pushed himself over to the driver's seat and maneuvered the car out onto the street, slid back to the passenger side and waited for Mother to enter.

Queen Alexandra was noted for her regal and graceful entrances into carriages, maintaining all the while her dignity as sovereign and mother of many. Perhaps it was not conscious on her part, but Mother imitated the queen down to the nod of the head and the lilt to the step. She opened the door and swept into the driver's seat with what can only be called majesty and splendor. Since the salesman was looking, he saw the hat coming and pushed himself to the far right of the seat and prepared his soul for the next phase.

Now this next phase I remember only sketchily, but it went something like this: Mother was a creature of habit and knew in her heart of hearts that gear shifts should be on the floor, although she was also aware that this car had the shift by the steering wheel. She took several practice runs at the new position and could not be faulted for her energy. The grinding of the gears did not trouble her and she did retain that part of habit wherein one used the clutch for shifting. So in a trice she was ready for the road.

She looked into the rearview mirror, made the proper

adjustments, and was as ready as pride and circumstance would make her. She pushed in the clutch but then habit took over. She grabbed for the shift where it should be — namely on the floor — and gave a masterful pull. Instead of the expected gear shift, she grabbed the salesman's knee, pulled it back and let up on the clutch.

Now several things happened at once: The salesman shrieked and scared Mother, who then looked over at the source of the disturbance and slashed his eye with the feathers on her hat. Immediately he put up his hands to defend himself from this onslaught and grabbed for the steering wheel. Why he did that and to what extent he was culpable is still a matter for the courts. What is very clear, however, is that Mother now had the car in first gear and we were in the street, but on the wrong side of the street as it turned out. The salesman was practically speechless, although he could be heard to whimper, "Lady, lady, lady." Mother's only comment was, "They shouldn't let children play in the streets."After a few swerves and false rightings, we were again on course. By now the salesman had his handkerchief out and was dabbing his bleeding left eye.

Mother had read somewhere that you could signal a turn from inside of the new cars. This would be known to later generations as the turn signal, but then it was still a new thing and on only some models— and not yet on the Studebaker. She asked as one looking for more than mere conversation, "Can you signal a turn without sticking your hand out the window?"

Perhaps the salesman did not understand the question or he was more interested in making the quick sale — although that was appealing to him less and less — that he said, "Yes, you could." So Mother figured that if you signaled from inside the car, there was no need for further manipulations, like stepping on the brake or turning the steering wheel. She released both hands from the wheel and began to wave her arms about and over her head like Don

Quixote doing his windmill thing. At the stop sign, cars on both our left and right screeched to a halt and watched as Mother gyrated in her rather strange body language that she intended to turn as per her directions to them. The car did not turn but sped blithely forward through the stop sign. The salesman was now in full whimper, "Oh, lady, lady, please, lady, oh, please lady."

I grew up with the full knowledge that Mother was never one to mollycoddle the weak in spirit. There was the time she fell down the 'L' platform steps, landed on her knees and lost her teeth. She stood up, reset the hat on her head, left her teeth on the pavement and trudged onward. That, to her, was showing Spirit. And she was not inclined to listen to some whimpering salesman, blithering over a little thing like the car not turning.

Perhaps, she thought, her signals were not large enough and would have to be made more emphatic. Why she thought saying "Uuuuuh, Uuuuuh" in a Wagnerian voice would do the trick remains speculation, but there is no dispute over the fact that she began to make larger gestures, much like those seen in rodeos at bull catching time, and bellowed "Uuuuuh, Uuuuuh." The salesman shut his one good eye and began his Act of Contrition.

Mother put the car in neutral, stepped on the brake and gas simultaneously and let the car come to rest in the middle of the next intersection, the engine revving noisily and importantly. "Is it broken?" she demanded. "Why didn't it turn?"

The salesman, fearing terrible repercussions if he were anything less than totally candid said, "That feature is not available on this model."

Mother said simply and magisterially, "Well, then." And for reasons I still do not understand, that seemed to settle the matter. She addressed me, although she was still looking fixedly at the windshield, "Let's get your Father."

The salesman did not know just exactly where this

supposedly easy sale stood and he was too frightened to ask. His eye had stopped bleeding for the most part, although his left leg was still fairly numb but he gamely hung in there and asked, "Is there anything else I can show you?"

"Yes," said Mother, "the windshield wipers."

Again on most cars, the windshield wipers are simple affairs with a switch that goes from off to medium to fast movements. On the Studebaker there were two switches, one on each side of the car. The salesman pointed to the switch in front of him and said, "Here it is, Ma'am." Mother ignored the switch in front of her and reached over to test the one in front of the salesman. He shrieked when he saw her lunge at him. "In front of you, in front of you," he hollered but to no avail. Mother continued her stretch to the passenger side of the car and brushed his cheek lightly with her feathered hat. He put his arms across his face and then buried his face in his hands, whether from terror or in protection I cannot say.

But it was the wrong gesture at any rate, for it was at this moment that the car got caught in the trolley tracks. The car began to swing on an axis not usually found in text books or in driving manuals and the salesman never saw the garbage truck directly in front of us. So Mother did what most mothers would do at such a juncture: she beeped the horn. I cannot remember if the beep came before or after the thud, but I do remember that they were very close together, quite possibly simultaneous. The sound of the horn had the effect of flushing a rabbit from its warren however, and the salesman peeked through his hands just in time to see us finish a perfect figure Eight in the middle of Madison Avenue. It was a thrill he had never before experienced and he was in speechless awe at the maneuver.

Mother, of course, acted as though the entire scenario had been prearranged and went quite according to plan. She jammed the car into first gear, gave it the gas, and shot off in the general direction of the showroom. She had decided that she had had quite enough test-driving for the day and it was time to go home. "Which way?" She demanded. The salesman pointed in some vague direction that indicated forward would do nicely, and since there were no other cars or garbage trucks ahead of us forward we went. And, except for the final game attempt Mother thought she should give the car to see if it really did not know how to turn when inwardly motivated, nothing exceptional happened.

By the time we arrived back at our starting point and Mother had pulled up neatly at the curb, Father had concluded the arrangements with the manager and the car was ours, insignificant dent and all. The salesman got out on the passenger side and limped backwards to the door as though in fear that Mother would follow him in, or worse yet offer to open the door for him. Father met us at the curb and Mother said, "Get in and I'll show you some of the thing-a-ma-jigs as we drive home."

This was to be the first of Mother's driving instructions in the Studebaker. There was, of course, the rather notable time she taught my older brother to drive. He has done very well in his therapy so I think I'll let him tell you about that some other time.

Photographic Memories

When you ask me to tell you about the places I have been, I easily remember the various hills and landscapes of a hundred different terrains and a thousand different scenes. And I remember the rooms which shared my secrets and my sleep, my communions and my disappointments. I can instantly remember where I was when I read this or that book, when I heard this or that bit of news or gossip.

I could tell you in striking detail about standing on a silent mesa and watching the full moon, its shape like a pregnant girl about to give birth to some new galaxy of stars, rise above the horizon and devour the darkness with almost unbearable light. I could tell you of the breeze that enfolds the creatures of the night and joins in ferocious unity enemies that, by day, would fight or flee in ancestral causes. I could tell you of suns that sear the blood and suck life from all plants and animals that inhabit an unfriendly plain.

But I do not think of a scene when asked for place. I think rather of the people who stand in front of a place and illumine that scene, much like a portrait photographed in black and white that dominates all the colors of the room in which it is displayed. And have you not noticed that? In a gallery of watercolors, oils, tempera, your eye is drawn instantly to the starkness of a black and white photograph which has captured a fleeting moment of history, which by its art has also captured the whole life of a human being, frozen in space and transcending all time? No color or amount of colors can hope to compensate for the expressed reality of a life that is brazenly set forth in the unforgiving, unrelenting presence of the total soul, exposed as it is to the admiration and jeers of both viewers and life.

The landscapes of my memory are much like that gallery. I am surrounded by muted shades of light and darkness. Events and circumstances have put me in surroundings that would be the envy of a Marco Polo or the scorn of a forgotten hermit. I could tell of assassinations and coronations, of being at historic speeches or at pivotal moments which defined our times. And they would all be true, but only to a point.

For you know, truth and fact are not always the same. We can have an indisputable fact presented before us and still may not know the truth. Or we can possess a truth that no fact can support, and yet we would die for that truth as we would never die for the fact. Facts are all the shades that may aid, or distract from, the truth. We acknowledge the facts for what they are and we are grateful for their importance. But we do not allow those facts to discourage truth.

And that holds equally for our memories. If we get lost in the labyrinth of either our minds or our facts, or if we confuse place with its reality, we will never know the exhilaration of watching the universe watch us. We will never enjoy the union of creation when the lion and the hunter, the fire and the rose, the tree and the hut, the child and grandfather all become one.

So my memories are not separate scenes. They are like the settings of a rare and precious photograph, which because of its beauty can hide itself in the face it embraces. They are there, but they do not intrude; they put into bold relief a face that is incomparable and breathtaking. So like all settings, because they are not seen they are beautiful.

I can even now see Maria Elena as she stands in front of her part-adobe, part-wood, part-shingle house. Each texture came at a different time but always with the same indifference to materials and contemporary style. Maria Elena was no less a slave to popular opinion than she was to those who would enslave her. The adobe section was the oldest part of the house. The straw could be seen mixed with the mud and the crumbling of the walls partly shrouded the single window that had not been opened for years. The turquoise coloring of the door frames and the window sills had long ago given up its luster and brightness to the searing sun and many rains. At some forgotten time, an attempt had been made to put screening on the windows and on the doors but that attempt had proven a failure just as the need for them had become less urgent.

In front of this weathered, used, and loved home stands Maria Elena. The first thing you would notice was that she had one, bright, crooked tooth which hung from her upper gums, encased between her pale red, almost rose-colored, lips. And is that not always the case? A musician hears the missed oboe note before he hears the whole of a Brahms symphony, the language teacher the mispronunciation of a word in a Verlaine poem, the mathematician the incorrect addition within a complex Newtonian formula before they ever hear the fullness of the music, the beauty of the poem, or the intricate complexities of the formula. We look for perfection in the world around us because we find ourselves so lacking in perfection in our ideals.

So was Maria Elena's single tooth in a face that would have caused an angel to weep for the sheer wonder at the stories that had left their marks and creases by their tales of disappointments weathered and dreams shattered. Those

152

distracted—rather than mesmerized— by that single tooth were the very ones who identified her as simply a woman, full of years, and they would have missed the incredible loveliness of the eyes. For her eyes held within them a wisdom that would never come from books and a passion that would never come from mere heroics. If her eyes had had a voice of their own, they would have told of adventures in the realm of life which would have to remain forever silent in the face of the great realities that neither books nor histories can relate.

And yet that one tooth also stood as a symbol of Maria Elena. It held on tenaciously as all its companions had been lost because of disease, or diet, or age. It could cling to its root because she refused to be conquered by either life or its trivialities. Her heritage was always present to Maria Elena, just as the mightiest oak clings to its roots for strength and stability throughout the hurricane, drought, or flood. Her ancestors lived in her bones as easily as her ancestors' bones lived in the cemetery on the hill outside of town.

You must understand that Maria Elena never once considered herself used by fate or rejected by life. She accepted tragedy with the same peaceful quiet with which she received delight. To her, life was neither friend nor foe but simply a force one acknowledged with grace and dignity, and occasionally with an unsuspected strength. She lived in a world created by a speechless Job without once giving into the temptation of justification or explanation. That world was created by a merciful but demanding God, and neither God nor Elena regarded the other with pity or indifference. She was never, not even for a single moment, unaware of God's presence and interest. She simply never wasted her time relating to her deity the tribulations of her day or the secret desires of her heart. She knew they were already known and therefore needed no diurnal recital to produce an intrusive effect. Life would be for her without shattering fatalism or empty optimism.

Maria Elena's smile was slight but highly revealing. She saw her own and life's incongruities as clever twists which displayed the foibles more than the follies of fate. There is no grand story to tell about Maria Elena. She is her own tale, its unfolding, and its meaning. She was as indistinguishable from the earth she stood on as she was from the house she stood in front of. And that is precisely the reason she is so memorable.

Her entire existence bespoke a compact unity, a power we can only imagine in times of frustrated desires or overwhelming horrors. Her very presence at the side of a bed filled with either birth or death was enough to give assurance that the journey — at either its beginning or at its end — would be sufficient proof that pettiness and meanness would have no place in her world or in the world around her. Maria Elena was a proud woman although she was not prideful. One saw in her eyes the unflinching determination to accept as a gift all that came to her, all that sustained her, and all that challenged her. Next to Maria Elena, I would place Gabriel. Him I would photograph as caged. Not the cages of a zoo or bird sanctuary, but the cages of the mind that hold in chains its inhabitants far better than could any bars of steel.

Gabriel would awake, as he knew he would, a full fifteen seconds before the alarm rang, signaling the beginning of another span of hours, minutes, seconds, of light and darkness, of hope and shadows. It was as though the clock itself enticed an intensity of expectation so that Gabriel's body, already expecting the summons, did not want to be found unprepared or unworthy of its daily assignation with hours, minutes, heat or chill. In that span of time between his eyes opening and the clock's summoning, Gabriel became fully alert, assured, whole and contained. His daily world existed only as something complete with only the hours or minutes to be experienced as they unraveled, bit by bit, tied to each other like finite links in an infinite chain. With automatic reaction, he interrupted the course of the clock's design so that no sound of the purposeful noise would bend the shape of the magic hour.

How does one account for that instant between sleep and wakefulness, between the counterfeit death and accustomed resurrection? Does it belong to the realm beyond the River Styx that one must cross again and again with no friendly hand or pinpoint of light for guidance? Or does it belong to a world, frozen both in thought and expectation, a world of silence beyond the unfathomable darkness? And how does an inhabitant of that instant know which it is?

Gabriel lived in each with perfect ease, never knowing the distress of its opposite. For him, sleep was dream-filled, inhabited by minotaurs and rocs who sported with satyrs and naiads; where innocence was indistinguishable from experience and merriment from sorrow, where the only reality was the sleep that gave that dream existence. He would not have been able to assign passion to his dreams any more than he could attribute indifference to his waking hours. The two worlds existed for him in that wholeness which only creation could imitate, but then only weakly. He may have been in awe of his dreams but he was never intimidated by them.

And who would dare to question dreams or spurn wakefulness? We may find our pain or fear circumscribed and limited by awareness of those pains or fears, but we cannot attribute our dreams to mendacity or duplicity. We each would not trade a single instant of a dream for a year of dreamless awareness of the surface that coats our actions and interactions. We shroud those actions so that they may become dreamlike and acceptable to us when the dream has been withheld or its meaning obscured.

For Gabriel, the dreams were not to be exposed to

anything other than their dreamlike existence. Nor were they to be sullied by comparison or scrutiny with a different standard of interpretation and experience. He would have fought with the strength of ten those who might tear from him a world he knew to be authentic, as unquestioned as it was perhaps unquestionable. And so it was that he left his minotaurs with their unseen and unbidden quests for his own accustomed services within the world of men. The ritual of ablutions and dressing which allied Gabriel to kings and peasants, to babes at birth and corpses at death, was accomplished with consummate skill and indifference. He cared no more for what covered his body than he did for the snow or sand which covered frozen tundras or burning deserts.

Breakfast was a useless meal to Gabriel as was lunch. These two meals, anticipated by others beyond their capacity to overlook, were for him wastes of time, effort, and energy. Only in the evening could he be said to feed at the table of common humanity, and then it was with just enough preparation as would be necessary to distinguish his dinner from the meals he had disdained earlier in the day. What gave Gabriel his sense of purpose was his dedication to duty, a duty that he felt reflected and circumscribed a world of perfect order and magnificent design.

Gabriel's first duty, as he saw it, was to be on time at the train depot where he would spend the next eight hours of his life. He had never boarded a train and he had never had the slightest desire to see where he would send his soldiers. For he saw the customers that line up in front of him at the ticket window as so many troops, waiting for an assignment into the unknown and hostile world of strife and conflict. But strife and conflicts were not part of Gabriel's concern.

To him, importance was found in giving to each person the correct piece of pasteboard which would permit travel to another station, or another city, or another world; it was all one to him. He never knew the name of a single customer and he had no desire to know. It was sufficient for him to see a face, know the face's destination, deliver a ticket to the hand below the face and then withdraw into his enclosure of comfort. Mornings were particularly busy times, but Gabriel could not be hurried or pushed into unseemly haste. Order could not be sacrificed for the thoughtlessness of others in making their preparations. If a train connection were missed, he could not be held responsible. Efficiency and correctness were, to him, of infinite importance and caused other concerns to pale. He did not have rhythms in his life. He had compartments— and no one segment would impinge on another, either in life or in destiny.

And so I would show Gabriel sitting in a cage which only others could see. His eyes would be expressionless and steady. No passion or disaster would shade those eyes, nor would love or discomfort penetrate them. Gabriel's soul was not small. It merely lacked human largeness. His eyes showed it and his cage proved it.

When I picture Mavis Alyred, I see a small figure, standing on a slight knoll in the middle of a windswept cemetery. Although she faces the photographer squarely, her face and stare are unflinchingly directed over his right shoulder at an object which only imagination could depict.

Widowhood became Mrs. Alyred in a way which surprised even her. She was quite accustomed to handling the intricacies of marriage with an ease and proficiency that led her to believe nothing was beyond her capacities to transform into an advantage another opportunity for assuming a deeper layer of power. Her rewards for keeping the house, for having the children, for seeing to their education and their reasonable acceptability in her own social circle, for providing the home-like touches which were the envy of her friends, all were a matter of deftness and expertness. These surrounded her as a shield against the cruelties of the world and the problems read about only in the papers or in novels that she never purchased. Mrs. Alyred's world did not provide for difficulties or contradictions. It was a simple, clean world that brooked no interference or challenge. And somehow, even though she had not planned on it, Mr. Alyred's death would have to fit into her scheme of life and genteel respectability. She was angrier at Mr. Alyred for dying without her permission than for actually dying. That was very inconsiderate of him because he knew how well she had managed him during their marriage.

Mr. Alyred's absence was not noticed at first. There was one less plate at the table; there was no waiting for use of the bathroom; there was one less load of washing every other day; there was a little less mail addressed to Mr. and Mrs.; but there was also no huge vacuum created by either loneliness or lack of companionship. There was a little less pressure to entertain during meals; a bit more time to spend with the Sunday paper. But, in general, neither the routine nor the pleasures were significantly dispensed with nor rearranged.

Mrs. Alyred had expected something more. She was not sure just what that more consisted in, but it seemed to her that she should at least have noticed Mr. Alyred's absence with an occasional pang of sorrow, or — if she could have managed it — a mild depression, perhaps just enough that a doctor would be called in to give her a pill or something. Mrs. Kindler had to see the doctor four times when Mr. Kindler died. Mrs. Alyred considered that excessive simply for the death of a husband. But maybe an initial visit from Doctor Higgins with one follow up would display the right amount of sorrow she expected from herself. The actual emotion was something far closer to a vague sense of a vacuum than a positive sense of a loss. She seemed to realize on her way home from Mr. Alyred's burial that a phase of her life had passed, been taken away from her without her consent and now was the time to play The Widow. Of course she felt up to it. She would manage the "doing beautifully" bit until she grew tired of it herself. She had played parts all her life from Sweet Child to Happy Wife to Dutiful Mother. Grieving Widow she did not feel would completely suit her, although Courageous Widow just might fit the bill. She knew at that instant that this would be her role until something less taxing came along.

Mr. Alyred's funeral was on a Wednesday. It was everything she had expected it to be, although there might have been just a bit too much praise for Mr. Alyred in the sermon. She who knew him better than anyone else in this world—after all, she was the Grieving Widow—who could have added much about his life and inability to cope without her. Mrs. Alyred would have been furious with the preacher if he had not found several kind things to say, but he should have mentioned in rather greater detail the way Mrs. Alyred had suffered her loss, the suddenness of it, and the sorrow of the family. She never considered the children in the family. They were there to give dimension to the relationship between husband and wife, not to absorb the condolences of others at the wake. There was that time they went on a camping trip and he could not even set the fire properly. Or the time... but there were so many times she would wait to recount them to others in the future as she had in the past. Mrs. Alyred had never asked either herself or her God if he had been a good man.

On Thursday she was back on the trail visiting the elderly and bringing them consolation and gossip. She could hear behind her back the accolades of her courage and strength. Although no one actually said it, she was sure she could hear the praise behind her back, "Have you noticed how beautifully Mavis is doing?" "She has such courage and all she thinks about is others." "Such a strong and wonderful woman."

"Doing beautifully" now became the hallmark of Mrs.

Alyred's demeanor. When she thought one of the parishioners was looking at her, she dabbed a soggy Kleenex in the corner of her eyes, the corner near the nose, and sniffled. She had no cold, but the sniffle seemed to give her a certain sense of authority and authenticity. Widows, Mrs. Alyred knew, wept, and so she wept without wasting the effort in private. Also weeping for her was a way to prove that her Doing Beautifully was setting a standard for the rest of the town widows to follow.

Only gradually did it dawn on her that Mr. Alyred's death had freed her to pursue other interests. She had always pestered the bed-ridden in their hospital rooms and overpowered the sickly in their homes. She continued to run the parish functions with a vigor and dedication that Attila the Hun would have envied and applauded. She still baked bread for those on a yeast-free diet and chocolate chip cookies for those on a diet. She did not let up her attendance at town council meetings to remind the representative she had never voted for that too much of the city money was being wasted on the poor who came through town. And, although she never paid taxes, she noisily demanded an accounting of the salaries paid to high school students for the work they did after school. Busy? Yes, but still she had time on her hands. And a Mavis Alyred with time on her hands was lethal.

What to do? How could she do beautifully in a wider area? How could she fill her days by doing good and reminding others of their evil? Now Mrs. Alyred was not a large woman. In face, she was rather small. Were some gift the gods given to her and she could have looked at herself in the mirror, she would have announced, "Common!" She did not think of herself as common however, for she was the very model of the good Christian woman that would eventually save the church from its headlong rush to disaster with communion in the hand. She had learned at an early age that frontal confrontations were

160

useless. Priests or mayors or school teachers always had ready answers to her objections and she knew she could not handle open confrontation and still retain her equanimity. In learning that open confrontation was useless, she also learned that subversion was one hundred percent effective. Further, she learned that stating that 'I heard' carried far more weight than 'Marilyn or Eleanor said.' So Mrs. Alyred, not a large woman, was always a Presence. Patients feigned slumber when they heard her knock on the hospital door, the homebound picked up their phones and talked to empty air at the sight of her, and cripples would have grown fleet of foot had it been possible.

As far as Mrs. Alyred was concerned, she was practicing what she had learned as a girl. On one Sunday the priest had said that we must think of others first. That was all she needed for the rest of her life and she never ceased thinking of others and what they should be doing, where they should be doing it, and with whom they shouldn't be doing it.

So Mavis should, I think, be photographed standing in the autumnal cemetery, the wind lightly brushing her grey hair. She would wear her black coat slightly opened, a black scarf, a black dress and she would face unflinchingly the fates, doing beautifully. She would have her right hand rest firmly upon a tombstone. And as she looked over the photographer's right shoulder, the granite of the tombstone would be only slightly softer than the glint in Mrs. Alyred's eye.

One of the strange phenomena we lose as we age is the ability to trust our intuitions. Have you not had the knowledge, just as the phone begins to ring, of the caller? And have you not begun to answer a question before the question is even asked? And who has not finished a sentence in words that exactly mimic the speaker's? We fear these intuitions and so teach ourselves to abandon them because they seem to separate us from our companions. We fear them because they speak to us of a world of the spirit which we cannot enter at will. They remind us of our ignorance of what is real and what is fantasy, and we are terrified in the face of that knowledge.

Jacob, however, neither doubted nor courted his intuitions. They were to him part of the world in which he lived with ease and in undisturbed communion. For this reason, I would not photograph Jacob's eyes but his hands. His hands were large for his size and reflected his soul more than his labors. For Jacob's hands were his intuition. His hands knew before he felt the seeds which crops would be fruitful and which would not. They could feel the amount of springtime rain that would be needed to make the soil fertile and lush. They knew just exactly the time for giving birth to a colt by caressing the underbelly of the mare. They recognized the amount of pressure to apply in birthing a calf and the exact moment when. His hands spoke to the animals in distress of their need to rely on him and not to fear. They knew just the softness to use when caressing a fretful child to sleep and the softness to use when laying the child quietly in the earth.

It was through the intuition of his hands that Jacob knew what was of value to be kept and what could be discarded with immediate forgetfulness. To him, a broken hoe that had embraced the earth was more valuable than a new hoe which had never felt the thrill of springtime planting. One touch of a plank of discarded wood told Jacob the many ways that plank could be used to mend a porch, or a step or a bedpost, how it could be used to straighten a twisted tree or support a sickly vine, how it could be placed in a crib or in a coffin. Indeed, Jacob's hands encompassed the whole world of dignity and so they were beautiful and they knew beauty in all its terrifying strength. Through them the universe conversed with him and he with his God. They knew the seasons and the fall of the stars far better than those who use barometers or telescopes. They were as strong as steel, they were as gentle as lamb's wool, they were as weathered as the wood on his barn, they were as firm as rock and as flexible as wheat.

Unforgiving or ignorant folks would say that Jacob had dirty hands and that they would never be clean. They would be right, of course. But they would, in their blindness, see only the surface and miss the whole meaning of Jacob's life as well as the unimportance of their own. Each callous and crease had been formed by a struggle that Jacob accepted as a gift from a benevolent god. Although those hands had never been folded in formal prayer, they had never ceased offering prayers of gratitude: gratitude for the drought as well as for the rains, gratitude for the seeds that would mold in the earth as well as for the seeds that would burst into a rich harvest, gratitude for the morning that separates and the evening that brings together, gratitude for the broken things of life as well as for the unities of a benign universe.

And so I would photograph Jacob's hands resting peacefully in his lap. One hand would be with the palm upward, perhaps indicating an acceptance or perhaps it would be a beckoning gesture to an unseen viewer to come and share some unnamed gift or bounty. The other hand would hang quietly with the fingers pointing gently down, relaxed as only those worthy of an engulfing tranquility are allowed to rest. And those hands would tell you more about Jacob than words ever could. Jacob's hands were the astonishing beauty of God touching Adam to birth. For the beauty of Jacob's hands was the beauty of life itself.

About the Author

Father George Reynolds, O.P. is a professed religious and priest of the Order of Preachers (St. Albert the Great Province, Chicago, USA). Raised in Oak Park and Maywood, Illinois, Reynolds earned his B.A. in philosophy from Aquinas Institute of Theology and his M.A. in English from the University of Dallas. With fifty plus years of ministry under his belt, his pastoral experience is extensive. Reynolds currently ministers at the Aquinas Newman Center in Albuquerque, New Mexico. This is his first book. When asked about his influences, Reynolds says his father was a master storyteller. He kept Reynolds and his siblings enthralled with stories told before bed.

"There's something satisfying about writing a short story and watching how it will end: it usually is a surprise."

1974363R00090

Made in the USA
San Bernardino, CA
25 February 2013